Girl Goddess #9

nine stories

Also by Francesca Lia Block

Weetzie Bat

Witch Baby

Cherokee Bat and The Goat Guys

Missing Angel Juan

Baby Be-Bop

The Hanged Man

Girl Goddess #9

nine stories by

Francesca Lia Block

Joanna Cotler Books
An Imprint of Harper Collins*Publishers*

"Winnie and Cubby" was previously published
in slightly different form as "Winnie & Tommy,"
© 1994 by Francesca Lia Block, in
Am I Blue? Coming Out from the Silence by
Marion Dane Bauer, HarperCollins Publishers, 1994.

"Blue," © 1996 by Francesca Lia Block, was previously
published in slightly different form in
When I Was Your Age, Candlewick Press, 1996.

"Tweetie Sweet Pea," © 1994 by Francesca Lia Block,
was previously published in *Soft Tar.*

Girl Goddess #9
Nine Stories

 Printed in the United States of America. For information address HarperCollins Children's Books, a division of HarperCollins Publishers, 10 East 53rd Street, New York, NY 10022.

Library of Congress Cataloging-in-Publication Data
Block, Francesca Lia.
Girl Goddess #9 : nine stories / by Francesca Lia Block
p. cm.
"Joanna Cotler books."
Contents: Tweetie Sweet Pea — Blue — Dragons in Manhattan — Girl Goddess #9 — Rave — The Canyon — Pixie and Pony — Winnie and Cubby — Orpheus.
ISBN 0-06-027211-2 — ISBN 0-06-027212-0 (lib. bdg.)
1. Short stories, American. [1. Short stories.] I. Title.
PZ7.B61945Gi 1996 95-52050
[Fic]—dc20 CIP
AC

Typography by Steve Scott
6 7 8 9 10

❖

Tweetie Sweet Pea for Megan and Erin

Blue for Charlotte

Dragons in Manhattan for Joanna

Girl Goddess #9 for Princess Robin

Rave for Teddy

The Canyon for Tori and Jenna

Pixie and Pony for Nicola

Winnie and Cubby for the Ducks

Orpheus for Teddy, too

and thanks to Gilda Block as always

Contents

Girl Goddess #9

nine stories

Tweetie Sweet Pea

In the morning, her mother helped her put on the bathing suit with the cartoon bird baby on it.

"You look just like Tweetie Bird," her mother said.

"Tweetie," she repeated.

She had tufts of white hair, big blue saucer eyes, a little round tummy and skinny arms and legs.

Her sister, Peachy Pie, came in.

"Doesn't she look just like Tweetie?"

Peachy Pie solemnly nodded.

"Go show your dad."

Peachy Pie took her sister's hand and they went through the apartment. It was an obstacle course of funny props that their father brought home from the studios—masks, models of cities, a robot, a suit of armor, marionettes, a giant stuffed spider in a web, a pair of angel wings. Outside it was so hot that the roses in the courtyard already smelled as sweet as if it were afternoon and the springer spaniels, Digger and Tugger, didn't leap up to greet the girls; they just beat their stubby tails on the sidewalk along with Ringo. The Beatles were playing on their father's boom box as he stood under the palm trees in front of the Spanish bungalow washing his Jeep.

"She's Tweetie," Peachy Pie said.

"She is!" said their father. He wiped his hands on a towel and kissed the tops of their heads.

"Spray us with the hose!" squealed Peachy Pie, and he did.

They giggled and wriggled in the rainbow water. Then Tweetie sat in a bucket and Peachy Pie wrapped a Snow-White-and-the-Seven-Dwarves towel around her. Tweetie liked the way it felt to fit her whole self into the bucket and watch her father washing his car. He wore baggy plaid shorts that hung low on his narrow hips and sunglasses that looked like two tiny old Beatles records.

"Time for breakfast, kidlets," their mother called.

Tweetie didn't want to get out of the bucket where she fit so perfectly. Her father had to pick her up, kicking and wiggling, and deliver her into a chair that was too big. She missed her bucket. She might not fit into it as well in a few days. Her mother brought bowls of oatmeal with bananas and honey.

Yuck, thought Tweetie. Too hot for oats. If she had been able to stay in the bucket she might have eaten them. She slid out through the back of the chair.

"Where are you going?" her father asked.

"Come sit back down and eat your breakfast like a big girl," said Peachy Pie as if she were the mother.

Tweetie ran across the blue-and-white kitchen floor to the refrigerator. She pulled on the door with both hands. She climbed inside, using the vegetable bins as stairs, and reached up. The bag of frozen peas hit her on the head as she fell backward onto the floor. It didn't hurt much but she cried anyway.

Her mother ladled her up.

"Now why did you do that?" her mother said, kissing the tufty top of Tweetie's head where her pink scalp showed through her hair.

"Peas," said Tweetie.

Her mother sat Tweetie on her lap and fed her

frozen peas until she stopped crying. Tweetie thought they tasted like candy, while unfrozen peas were mushy and not as sweet. She tried to offer some to her mother, her father and Peachy Pie, but no one wanted any.

"Tweetie Sweet Pea," her father said. And that was how she got her name.

After breakfast Tweetie Sweet Pea and Peachy Pie played Beauty and the Beast because it was Peachy Pie's favorite game. Tweetie always had to be the Beast. Peachy Pie always got to be Beauty. Tweetie could have complained, but she never did because it seemed to mean a lot to Peachy Pie to be Beauty. Tweetie contemplated the fact that she and Peachy Pie were blonds, while their mother and Beauty had luscious brown curls. She thought that her father and the Beast must especially like brown hair. Her own hair was, as everyone had pointed out today, the color of a baby bird. Her grandmother had called it floozy blond, which wasn't, she gathered, a particularly good thing.

"You be the Beast," Peachy Pie said.

Tweetie thought, Oh surprise surprise.

She held the Beast doll and made him hop

around. He had a hairy head with horns and tusks, a padded back, soft paws and a bushy tail. Tweetie thought he was cute like that. She wished that Peachy Pie would let him keep his Beast outfit on.

Peachy Pie took off Beauty's plain blue dress. It was hard to get it off over her pointy plastic breasts, hard plastic hands and steep plastic where-are-my-pumps feet.

Peachy and Tweetie examined naked Beauty. She sure looked different naked than they did.

"I'll put on her married dress," Peachy Pie announced.

She opened the ballerina music box and took out the gold lamé ball gown, closing the box before the music started to play. Tweetie always hated the fakey-sweet smell of that dress. Peachy put it on Beauty.

"Okay. Now we dance," Peachy instructed.

She opened the music box again. This time a little twinkling tinkling song flew out of it like a fairy. The ballerina spun on one pink toe in front of her mirror. Tweetie Sweet Pea held the Beast up to Beauty and they danced. Everything got very still except for the tune playing over and over. A light breeze came in through the window, warm and rosy.

"Now ask me to marry you," Peachy Pie told Tweetie as she danced Beauty.

Peachy Pie's teeth showed when she was bossy. They reminded Tweetie of Dig's and Tug's tiny front teeth that she could see when she pulled their dog lips back.

"Will marry me?" asked Tweetie Sweet Pea.

"No. Say it like this," and Peachy Pie growled the words.

"Will marry me?" squeaked Tweetie again.

Peachy Pie rolled her eyes. "No. Not unless you take off your clothes."

"No," said Tweetie.

Peachy Pie got mad. She took the Beast away from Tweetie and undressed him. Under his Beastly costume Tweetie thought he was dumb-and-naked-looking. The only good thing about him was his hair. It was nice and long like their father's. When their father had seen it he had said, "I don't remember my sister's Ken doll ever having such long locks. It must be a grunge Ken."

"He's not Ken. He's the Beast," Peachy Pie told him.

"Oh, that explains it," he laughed.

Sometimes their father wore his hair in a ponytail. Sometimes he let it out and Tweetie played with it. It was blond like hers, and like Beast's. Sometimes he grew a goatee which made him look a lot like Beast, but Tweetie wouldn't have told him that. It might have hurt his feelings.

Their mother came in wearing a blue flowered sundress and her big, clunky, lace-up boots. She looked like Beauty except for the shoes.

"What's going on?" she said, squatting down next to them.

"The prince is marrying me," Peachy said.

"Now you girls shouldn't expect a handsome prince to come along and make it all better. I grew up on those fairy tales and it didn't do me any good."

Tweetie thought, Just let Peachy Pie enjoy her handsome prince. It makes her happy. Besides, you did find a prince.

When her father held her it made everything all better, just for then, but all better for then was pretty good. No one had to tell her and Peachy Pie that not all fairy tales come true. They knew more than they let on.

"Time to get dressed and go to the park," their Beauty-mama said.

She put Tweetie in the red wagon. Their father walked behind with Dig and Tug. The dogs' butts swung low to the ground and their tails beat Beatles' rhythms as they competed to see who could pee in more places. Peachy Pie led the whole procession on her pink tricycle.

Tweetie pointed to flowers on the way and her mother picked them and put them in the wagon. Red bottlebrush, yellow daisies, hibiscus like hula girls wore.

"You are a flower, Tweetie Sweet Pea," her mother said, tucking a hibiscus behind Tweetie's ear.

At the park Tweetie and Peachy Pie went searching for elf homes. Elves liked the darkest, dampest, most overgrown places. Tweetie and Peachy pushed back the foliage and hid under the leaves. Tweetie thought she could see elves leaping from leaf to flower. You couldn't see them straight on, but you could glimpse them from the side. They had tilted eyes and sharp little teeth like Peachy Pie's. They could play music like the Beatles, only much higher and softer so that only Tweetie and Peachy could hear. They got drunk on flower nectar and fell asleep in the dirt, so you had to be careful not to squish one. If you made too much noise they scratched you with their long fingernails and put sand in your panties.

"Oh wow, where are my girls?" they heard their father say.

Peachy put her finger to her lips.

"I'm really worried. Maybe someone took them away. Maybe they decided to leave me. I'll never recover."

Tweetie squirmed, but Peachy held her still.

"I hope they come back soon. My heart is broken."

Those were the magic words. Tweetie and Peachy giggled.

"Sounds like elves," their father said.

They giggled louder. He came closer. They saw his feet through the leaves. He had broad tan feet that reminded Tweetie of her stuffed lion's paws. Beast feet.

"Elves, do you know where my babies are?"

He bent down. They saw his eyes peering over the top rim of his sunglasses. Each eye was as full of mystery and blue-green magic as an elf itself.

"Look who's here," he said. "Boy am I glad I found you! I've come to escort you to the picnic."

They crawled out of the elf home and took his hands. The picnic was organic grapes (the only kind you were allowed to have because of the farm-workers), almond butter sandwiches on bagels, and lemonade. Tweetie wanted her frozen peas, but she ate the grapes instead to make her mother happy. You had to do a lot of things for that reason.

When they got home that evening Tweetie's shoulders felt hot from the sun, and the sand in her pants was scratchy. She must have made too much noise in the elf home, she thought. It had been because of her father—she had had to let him know where she was; his heart would have broken without her.

Their mother gave the girls a bath in the lavender-and-white tiled bathroom, shampooing their hair into unicorn horns with No More Tears.

"The bad men can't get us now," Peachy Pie said.

"What bad men?" asked their mother.

"The *bad* men. But we're safe because our horns have power."

"There aren't any bad men," their mother said.

Tweetie knew this was a lie. There were bad men. Just like there were princes, elves and magic horns. They created weapons that could destroy the earth, they tore down the healing elf forests, they didn't take care of people who were sick and hungry.

Later, Tweetie and Peachy Pie, smelling of No More Tears and baby powder, curled up with their father on the sofa while he watched the evening news. A singer had shot himself in the head. He looked like Tweetie's father.

Tweetie's mother gasped. Her father lifted his hand off Tweetie's head and took her mother's hand.

When Tweetie was tucked in bed she heard her mother say, tears in her voice, "They had a good summer day."

"To these girls every day is summer. Luckily. I wish they never had to figure out about winter," their father said softly, stroking Tweetie's head.

But Tweetie Sweet Pea already knew that she would outgrow her Tweetie Bird bathing suit, outgrow her bucket. She knew that the winter would come, cold gray-and-white static like the TV screen between chattering color, droning death like the newscaster's voice.

She held her summer day in her arms like a Beast prince, warm, enchanted, and real as any sadness, as she fell asleep.

Blue

La thought it was strange that her mother had named her La since La's mother hated the city where she lived. Maybe, La thought, her mother had named her that for a different reason but she didn't know what. She asked her father who shrugged and said, "She was always dreaming, fantasizing. I wanted to name you Lisa."

La hoped the name came from one of her mother's dreams about music.

"I dreamed I heard the most celestial melody," La's mother would say. "There were angels in the room. They were dressed in black with gold and silver wings."

La didn't mind that kind of fantasy, only the other ones that had made her mother cry and scream, gesturing wildly, telling La to shut the closet door so no one could get out, talking to people who were not there. Only the ones that had sent her mother away.

* * *

La sat on the lawn and watched mothers gathering their children. When the sun started to go down she walked home along the broad streets lined with small houses and magnolia trees, their thick, white, leaflike blossoms crisping brown at the edges. The air smelled of gasoline, chlorine and fast-food meat with an occasional whiff of mock orange, too faint to disguise much with its sweetness.

La walked up the path, under the birch tree that shivered in the last rays of sun, and went into the condominium. She found her father sitting in the dark drinking from a bottle of whiskey.

"Daddy?" she whispered. He looked up and his unshaven face with the red eyes made her step backward as if she had been hit.

"She figured out a way," he said. It sounded like there was a wad of wet tissue in his throat.

La remembered the blood in the bathtub. She hadn't thought someone could lose so much blood and still be alive. Her mother had been lying slumped on the floor and La had run screaming to get her father.

Had her mother done that again? There in the hospital where they were supposed to protect her? La wondered if someone had told her to do it—one of the voices in her head. This time La had not been there to come in and see the blood and save her.

"What happened?" La asked.

"I just told you." He never raised his voice to her. "She killed herself."

La took a step toward her father, but the look in his eyes made her back away into her bedroom and shut the door.

She sat on her bed and stared at the peach-colored wall. She had helped her mother paint it.

"Peach is soothing," her mother had said.

Now it made La sick to her stomach. She looked at Emily, H.D., Sylvia, Anne, Christina and Elizabeth sitting in the love seat. Her mother had named them after her favorite poets. They stared back with blank, glassy doll eyes.

La wanted to cry but she couldn't. She felt like a Tiny Tears doll with no water inside.

"La," said a voice.

She jumped and turned around. The closet door was open a crack. La never left the closet door open. She was afraid that demons would come out and get her in the night. Once when her mother was very upset, she had told La about the demons that lived in closets.

"La," the voice whispered.

She held her breath.

The closet door opened a little more and a tiny shadow tiptoed out.

Maybe, she thought later, Blue was really just her tears. Maybe Blue was the tears that didn't come.

The creature came into the light. It had thin, pale, slightly bluish skin. It blinked at La with blue eyes under glittery eyelashes.

"Who are you?" La felt a slice of fear, remembering her mother's tub full of blood. Had her mother seen this creature? Had this been the demon who told her mother to cut herself?

The creature shrugged.

"Why are you here?"

"To be your friend."

La rubbed her eyes. "Are you some kind of closet demon?"

The creature looked about to cry. La shook her head, trying to make it go away.

"Now you should sleep, I think." And the creature reached out tiny blue fingers with bitten nails and touched La's forehead.

Almost immediately, she was asleep.

She dreamed about the creature holding her mother's hand and running through a field of cornflowers.

"Blue," La's mother said in the dream. "Your name is Blue."

After the children at school heard about La's mother, they avoided La as much as possible and whispered about her when she walked by. La always felt as if they could see stains on her clothes or smell odors on her body. She came home after school to the dim condo. The curtains were drawn and the only light was the television's glow. La's father had stopped going to work. He stayed home every day and drank and watched talk shows and reruns.

La fixed herself a bowl of cornflakes and went into her room to talk to Blue. Mostly they talked about La's mother.

"I can tell you things about her," Blue said.

"How do you know?" La was suspicious. Did this mean that Blue had been one of the voices in La's mother's head?

"I know because I know you and you understood her more than you think."

"Like what do you know?"

"She wrote poetry. She wanted to go to New York City and study poetry."

La thought about the sketchbooks with the thick, bumpy, black covers that her mother used for writing poetry in. She had tried to find them the day after her mother died but her father had hidden them or thrown them away. La was afraid to ask him. There had always been something almost forbidden about her mother's poetry. La tried to remember some of it. Once she had opened a tiny bottle of French perfume that was sitting on her mother's marble-top dressing table. As she breathed in the orange blossoms she remembered something about a girl dancing in a garden while a black swan watched her with hating eyes and something about a woman with black roses tattooed on her body. Something about a blue child calling from out of the mists—begging.

"Why didn't she go to New York?" La asked.

"She stayed here because of your dad."

"Did she love him?"

"She loved him. But she knew he would never understand her."

La knew that her mother had met her father in her high school English class. He was the teacher. When La's mother graduated, La's father called her up and asked her to the opera. Even though he was older, La's mother found him attractive. He had a strong chin and kind eyes and he knew about literature. La's mother wanted to go back east to college, but she decided to stay with La's father in his condo in the San Fernando Valley after her own mother died. They got married when she found out she was pregnant with La.

"Did she want me?" La asked Blue.

"At first she was scared of you. You were so red and noisy and she felt like you kept taking from her. She didn't have much extra to give to you because she was really still a kid herself."

La could feel her eyes stinging, but Blue said, "Then she changed her mind. After a while you were all she really cared about."

"Then why did she leave?"

Blue went and perched on the windowsill. "That I don't know," Blue said.

One day at lunch Chelsea Fox came and sat next to La. Chelsea had shiny, lemonade-colored hair tied up high in a ponytail and she was wearing pink lip gloss that smelled like bubble gum. La thought she was beautiful. She made you want to give her things.

"Don't you have any friends?" Chelsea demanded.

La shrugged.

"Why not?"

La said, "I like to play by myself."

"I used to be that way," Chelsea said. "I started talking when I was real little, and the other kids didn't understand what I was saying. They just sat in the sandbox and stared at me. So I made up an imaginary friend I talked to. But my mother told me it wasn't healthy."

"I do have one friend." La had been wanting to talk about Blue so much. And now Chelsea Fox was asking! La's heart started to pound against her. She felt as if she were made of something thin and breakable with this one heavy thing inside. "Blue is blue and lives in my closet."

Chelsea laughed, all tiny teeth like mean pearls. "You still have an imaginary friend?"

"Blue is real."

Chelsea made a face at La, flipped her hair, picked up her pink Barbie lunch box and walked away. La crushed her brown paper bag with her fist on the lunch table where she sat alone now. Milk from the small carton inside seeped onto the peeling scratched table and dripped down.

After that no one talked to La at all. Every day she came straight home from school and went to her room to see Blue and tell about her day.

One day La had walked into her English class and seen a boy slumped in the back of the room. His brown curly hair fell over his eyes. His skin was very tan as if he had spent the whole summer at the beach. He was scowling, doodling on the desk, but when Chelsea walked in he looked up and smiled. His name was Jason Court. At lunch, La saw him walking with his arm around Chelsea Fox.

"They are so beautiful," La told Blue.

"They sound kind of dopey to me."

"What do you mean?"

"She was nasty to you, remember?"

Blue looked away from La, and she wondered if she had hurt Blue's feelings. Blue was very sensitive. Blue said you could tell how sensitive someone was by their hands, and Blue's hands were long and thin, like La's mother's had been, with tapering fingertips. La had not noticed Jason Court's or Chelsea Fox's hands.

"Blue?" La said. "Are you okay?"

"You sound like you have a crush on both of them," Blue sniffed.

"Not *on* her. I want to *be* her."

"Oh, sure."

"What is that supposed to mean?"

"Never mind."

"Blue, what is your problem?"

"I just don't know if you're sure if you like girls or boys."

"You should talk. I think you don't even *know* if you are a girl or a boy." La turned her back on Blue and began to unbutton her denim shirt. She took it off and looked at herself in the mirror. She was wearing a white undershirt and her nipples showed through. Her breasts were very small, almost nonexistent.

"I wish my mom was alive to take me bra shopping," she said.

"Listen to you!" Blue scolded. "Bra shopping! That's why you want her back? You sound like one of those stupid girls at your school."

"That's not what I mean. Shut up, Blue."

It was the first time La had told Blue to shut up. She crossed her arms on her chest and looked into Blue's strange pale eyes. Suddenly she hated

Blue. Who was this creature, always hanging around here talking to her, keeping her from going out and making friends? Maybe it was Blue's fault that La's mother was dead. La could smell her own sweat—salty and sour. She wasn't a clean-smelling little girl anymore. Her mother's perfume bottles were all empty. She would have to go to the drugstore and get some deodorant like the teacher had talked to the girls about today.

"What are you anyway, Blue?" La said. She felt greasy and hot. She hated herself. Chelsea Fox and Jason Court would never be friends with her.

Blue said meekly, "I'm just Blue."

"Take off your clothes," said La. She felt mean. She wanted to crush Blue's sensitive fingers.

Blue had always worn the same baggy blue-and-white-striped pajamas, tiny blue feet sticking out from the bottom. Blue stared at La.

"Okay!" Blue said. "Okay, La, you asked for it. You wanted to see. But remember, after this, that's it. I'm not coming back."

"Fine!" La said. "I don't want you anyway. You are a creep. I want real, beautiful friends like Jason Court and Chelsea."

Blue unbuttoned the pajama top. Blue had little breasts.

"So you are a girl," La said. She stared at Blue's breasts which were really quite beautiful, smaller versions of what Chelsea Fox's bare breasts might have looked like.

Blue slipped out of the pajama bottoms.

"Oh!" La said. Blue was not just a girl. Blue was both.

"Good-bye, La," Blue said.

La went to her parents' bedroom and sat in the closet, burying her face in the hems of dresses and feeling the soft dark fabrics against her cheeks.

She heard the closet open. She held her breath. Her father was standing there holding an empty bottle of whiskey. He put his arms around a sheer black dress with pink roses on it. He started to cry—painful almost inhuman-sounding gasps. La tried not to move. She was afraid that her father would rip all the dresses off their pink satin hangers and throw them in the Dumpster or set fire to them. But after a while her father turned, and shuffled away.

Chelsea Fox had a birthday party. La saw the invitations with the ballerinas on them. She waited and waited. But she was the only girl who didn't get one.

When Miss Rose found out she asked La and Chelsea to stay after school. Miss Rose was a very thin, freckled, red-haired woman who always wore shades of green or pink.

"Chelsea, don't you think you should invite La to your birthday party?" Miss Rose said.

La looked down to hide her red face. She remembered what Blue had told her about how red she had been as a baby, how it had frightened her mother.

Chelsea shrugged.

"Go ahead, Chelsea, ask La. It isn't nice to leave her out."

Chelsea smiled so her small, white teeth showed. They reminded La of a doll's. "La, would you like to come to my party?"

La was afraid to look up or move. She hated Miss Rose then.

"She doesn't want to," Chelsea said.

"I think she does," said Miss Rose. "Don't you, La?"

"Okay," La whispered, wanting her teacher to shut up.

"Just don't bring any imaginary friends," Chelsea hissed when they were dismissed onto the burning asphalt. La imagined Chelsea spitting her teeth out like weapons. The air smelled grimy and hot like the pink rubber handballs.

La walked past some boys playing volleyball. The insides of her wrists were chafed from trying to serve at recess, her knees were scraped from falling down in softball, her knuckles raw from jacks. Sometimes her knees and knuckles were embedded with bits of gravel, speckled with blood. She had mosquito bites on her back. She felt as if the boys could see stains on her clothes or smell odors on her body.

"There goes Wacko," one of the boys shouted.

La felt chafed, scraped, raw and bitten inside too, and there was no one to go home and tell.

La wasn't planning to go to Chelsea Fox's birthday party but she saved the invitation anyway. La's father saw it. He hardly spoke to his daughter anymore, but that morning he said, "Is that a party invitation?"

La nodded.

"Good," said her father. "It's about time you did something like that."

La went mostly because her father had seemed

interested in her again and she wanted to please him, she wanted him to see her, but the next weekend when he drove her to Chelsea's tall house with the bright lawn, camellia-filled garden, the balloons tied to the mailbox and the white BMW in the driveway, he was as far away as ever.

Maybe it is better that he doesn't offer to walk me in, she thought. I don't want them to see him anyway.

She wanted to go home and try to find Blue but instead she jumped out of the car and went up to the door where a group of girls waited with their mothers.

Chelsea answered, wearing a pastel jeans outfit. The girls kissed her cheek and gave her presents. When it was La's turn, she gulped and brushed her lips against Chelsea's face. Chelsea reached up to her cheek and rubbed away the kiss with the back of her hand.

Inside, the house was decorated in huge chrysanthemum prints and lit up with what seemed like hundreds of lamps. Little pastel girls were running around screaming. There was one room all made of glass and filled with leafy, white iron furniture and plants. In the middle was a long table heaped with presents. La sat in a corner of the room by herself. After a while, Chelsea's mother came in leading a chorus of "Happy Birthday" and holding a huge cake covered in wet-looking pink-frosting roses. Chelsea's mother had a face like a model on a magazine cover—cat eyes, high cheekbones, full, pouting lips. She was tall and slender, her blond hair piled on top of her head with little wisps brushing down against her long, pearled neck. La watched Chelsea blow out eleven candles in one breath.

"I'll get my wish!"

She probably did get her wish, La thought, watching Chelsea's small hands tearing open the presents—Barbies, Barbie clothes, Barbie cars, stuffed toys, jeans, T-shirts, a glittery magenta bike with a white lattice basket covered with pink plastic flowers.

La had brought the almost-empty bottle of perfume that had belonged to her mother. Even though the fragrance inside it was the only thing that seemed to bring La's mother back, La had decided to give it to Chelsea. Maybe it would make Chelsea like her, La thought. It was her greatest treasure.

When Chelsea opened it she said, "What's this? It's been used!" and threw it aside.

La waited for the sound of it shattering, like her tiny glass tossed-off heart.

Chelsea's mother let the girls stay up until midnight, and then she told them to get their sleeping bags. La's belonged to her father—blue with red-flannel ducks on the inside. The other girls had pastel sleeping bags with Snow White or Barbie on them. La put her bag down in a corner and listened to the sugar-wild giggles all around her.

Suddenly she heard Chelsea say, "La, tell us about your imaginary friend. La has an imaginary friend."

La said, "No I don't."

"She gave you an imaginary present," said Amanda Warner.

Snickers. They sounded mean with too much cake. La was silent.

"Come on," the girls squealed. "Tell us."

"She can't help it," said Katie Dell. "She takes after her mother."

La buried down in the musty red flannel of her sleeping bag.

Blue, she thought, to keep herself from crying.

Near morning when the other girls were finally quiet, warm, thin arms the color of Chelsea Fox's eyes wrapped around La's waist.

"Write about it," Blue whispered. "Write it all."

That was the same thing Miss Rose said the next day in class. "I want us all to write about someone we love." She looked straight at La. La noticed for the first time how sad Miss Rose's brown eyes were.

La went home and shut the door of her room. She lay down on her belly on the floor with a pen and a piece of paper. There was a creaking sound and the closet door opened. Blue came out.

"I'm sorry, Blue," La said.

Blue sniffed. "What are you doing?" Blue asked.

"I'm supposed to write about someone I love. I want to write about my mom, but I'm afraid."

Blue began to whisper things in La's ear. She picked up her pen and wrote.

La wrote about her thin, elegant mother who always wore beautiful black French clothes and hid wet eyes behind large black cat glasses. La's mother liked to rent sad movies and cry so that she would not have to hide the tears that always seemed to be waiting to pour out. La wrote about her mother's thin hands with the nails manicured "French style"—peachy pale with white tips. The hands were never still—scribbling in notebooks, arranging bunches of gladioli and lilies, touching her dark hair, rubbing her own lipstick stains off of La's cheeks. La wrote about the flowery, citrusy perfumes her mother brought home from the department store cosmetic counter where she worked—tiny vials with pale, sunbeam-colored liquid on the inside and French names. Sometimes La's mother made La up with red lipstick and black eyeliner so they looked like sisters.

La's mother told La a secret: working in the department store was not what she really wanted; what she really wanted was to be a writer. Once in a while she would read her poetry out loud to her daughter. La hadn't understood much but she remembered the soothing sound of her mother's voice and the poem like perfume making a cloud around them.

La felt the secret of sadness bonding them together then.

"I will love you forever," La's mother had said. "No matter where I am, I am always loving you."

La remembered, when she was a little girl, how her mother had held her close and said, "Can you see the little dolls in Mommy's eyes?" La had seen two tiny Las there. As she got older she still looked for herself inside her mother. Now she tried to find that La in her father, but his eyes were closed to her, dull and blind.

La wrote about all of that and about the perfume bottle shaped like a teardrop that had brought her mother back.

"This is wonderful, La," Miss Rose said. "Would you like to read it to the class?"

La shook her head, cringing, pressing her back against hard wood and metal.

"I really think you should," said Miss Rose.

Chelsea Fox said, "I'd love to hear your story." She said it so sweetly that for a moment La believed her. But then she saw Chelsea glance over at Amanda Warner and a silent laugh swelled the air between them.

"Go ahead," Miss Rose said.

La couldn't breathe. She felt like throwing up.

But when she started to read, something happened. She forgot about Chelsea Fox, Jason Court, Amanda Warner and everyone else in the class. The words La and Blue had written cast their spell—even over La. She could smell the perfume; she could feel her mother's fingers wiping the lipstick stains off her cheek, then feel her mother's lips kissing her again in the same place, hear her mother laughing.

When La was finished she looked up. Everyone was silent, watching her.

"That was beautiful," Miss Rose finally said.

The bell rang and the class scattered. La went into the fluorescent-lit, brown and beigy-pink hallway. Her heart was beating fast but in a different way this time. She felt as if she had physically touched everyone in the room, as if she had let Jason Court stroke a dress of black crepe de chine, lifted an open, tear-shaped bottle of fragrance to Chelsea Fox's face.

"Your mom sounds like she was cool," Chelsea said, catching up with La. "My mom never said anything like that to me." La looked into Chelsea's blue eyes. The pupils were big and dark. There was no laughter in them now. La nodded.

Chelsea tossed her hair and ran off.

When La got home she ran inside to tell Blue. Her father wasn't on the couch watching TV where La expected him. She heard his typewriter keys and peeked into his office. The windows were open and Vivaldi was playing; he had a cup of coffee at his fingertips.

"Daddy," La said.

When she handed him the story his eyes changed.

"It's about Mom," La said, but she knew he knew.

"I'm writing something about her, too," he said. He held out his hand and she went to him. He leaned over and kissed her forehead.

"Thank you, honey." He looked like he hadn't slept or eaten for days. But he took off his glasses then, and La saw two small images of herself swimming in the tears in his eyes.

La went to her room to tell Blue. In the closet there were only clothes and shoes and shadows now.

Dragons in Manhattan

Manhattan

My name is Tuck Budd. I live in Manhattan with Izzy and Anastasia. The thing about Manhattan is that everything is here, all mixed together, that's what I love about it. Ugly things and beautiful things you didn't even think could exist. It's loud and dirty, our apartment is teeny and you have to walk up eight flights to get to it but we have a fireplace with carved angels, a leopard-print chaise lounge, Maxfield Parrish prints of nymphs in classical sunset gardens, pink-damask drapes and silk roses in platform shoes from the 40's and 70's that Izzy has collected. Izzy grows real roses in pots on the fire escape. She loves flowers and is always teaching me the names of different ones. She especially likes the ones with really ugly names. Anastasia grows oregano, dill, parsley and basil on the fire escape. She uses them in her special inter-international recipes. Anastasia believes you should never be afraid to mix cultures. She makes a Japanese-Italianish miso-pesto sauce for pasta and a bright-pink tandoori tofu stir-fry. I can tell what she's making just by sniffing the air. Sometimes when Anastasia doesn't feel like cooking, she and Izzy and I go to our favorite restaurants. We have golden curried-vegetable samosas and yogurt-cucumber salad under trees filled with fireflies in the courtyard of our favorite Indian restaurant. We have fettuccine at an Italian place where the Mafia guys used to shoot each other while they were sucking up pasta. We like the pink and green rice chips and the rose petals in the salad with the peanut dressing and the ginger tofu at our Thai place. There is a Middle Eastern restaurant we go to where you can get minty tabbouleh and yummy mushy hummus in pita bread for really cheap, and a funny Russian restaurant with bright murals of animals in people clothes dancing around cottages in the countryside. We eat borscht there, and drink tea from a silver samovar.

At night, after dinner, if Izzy isn't in a show or waitressing at the bar, we all sit together on the chaise lounge or the angel tapestry cushions, and Anastasia makes dresses for Izzy or strings her rosary-bead jewelry and Izzy who is an actress reads out loud from our favorite books, *The Wind in the Willows, The Animal Family, Alice in Wonderland, Siddhartha, The Prophet* and *Goodnight Moon*. Sometimes, instead of reading, Izzy makes up stories about fairies. She tells about water spirits and tree spirits and how they are sad because they have to live in human-looking bodies, but their true bodies are oceans and pools or birch trees or oak trees. I look at Anastasia with the light making the diamond in her nose sparkle and the roses made of quartz, silver or wood filling her hands. I look at Izzy with her long legs wrapped so many times around and her hair like Central Park in autumn. I hear her gorgeous voice filling up our world.

I am a lot like Anastasia because I know about herbs and food and I have a turned-up nose, a sharp chin and little fingers that can do things like stringing beads. I am a lot like Izzy because I like to perform and talk a lot and have red hair. I am so much like both of them that I never think about which one is my mom. They are both my mom.

Sometimes Izzy and Anastasia and I walk all over the city. We go to the Museum of Modern Art and stand in front of the paintings and tell each other how we feel.

"Rothko makes me calm," says Izzy. "But actually I prefer Maxfield Parrish, if you want to know the truth."

Anastasia tugs on whatever she can manage to grab of her own short hair when she looks at Pollock.

I say, "Klee makes me happy, like doing cartwheels."

Sometimes we walk or do cartwheels through Central Park and discover things; we find fortresses where we do scenes from Shakespeare. We sit under the angel at the edge of the fountain and do scenes from our favorite play, *Angels in America*, that we have seen so many times that we almost know it by heart. Izzy gets free tickets; she is friends with everybody. We buy lemonades and pretzels from the vendor carts. We go to pay our respects at the mosaic that says "Imagine." Many countries contributed stones to it. It is for John Lennon, who lived and died at the Dakota, which is a tall building at the edge of the park. There are dragons all around it. Izzy knows all about John Lennon. She says the Dakota got its name because a bunch of rich artsy New Yorkers wanted to leave the east side and start a new community "as remote as the Dakotas." John Lennon and Yoko Ono lived on a whole floor of the Dakota. Once on John Lennon's birthday, Yoko and Sean came out with a birthday cake for all his fans. I think that is brave and also very generous and forgiving after John Lennon had been killed. Izzy held me up so I could see. Yoko had a face like the moon. Her voice is like stars, ice and fire. I think Izzy and Anastasia love each other as much as John and Yoko did. Sometimes Izzy brings her boom box to the Imagine mosaic and plays a John or Yoko song and I dance.

I take modern dance three times a week from Natasha Horowitz, who is supposed to be almost a hundred years old. Her cheekbones remind me of a bird with its wings spread. We wear black leotards and tights without feet. After class the bottoms of my feet are always the color of my dance clothes from the wooden floor. We dance to live drums. Natasha Horowitz flies around the room like the bird in her cheekbones, beating a drum and crying out, "Express your soul, Essence!" She says it in a way so that I used to think she was talking to a kid named Essence in the class, because all the kids have pretty unusual artsy names like Melody and Phaedra and my friend Jasmine. Their parents are bohemian types like Izzy and Anastasia. But she was talking to all of us: "Express your soul-essence."

Even though I am the tiniest one I am pretty good. Dancing never seems hard to me. It is just what my body likes to do. Izzy says it's because I am a very centered child. I think it is because Izzy and Anastasia always made me feel like I could be good at whatever I liked to do. Once we were on a bus, and there was a girl my age with her pinched-mouth grandmother. The little girl was happy and chattering about how when she grew up she wanted to be "an actress or a writer or a dancer or a violinist." The grandmother said, "Oh no, you're too old to be a dancer or a violinist. You would have had to have started years ago when you were little. You'll never make it now. And you're too short to be a dancer besides." That got to me since I'm smaller than the girl was. "What about a writer or an actress?" she asked. You could tell she felt really bad. "It is almost impossible to be successful as a writer," the grandmother said. "And you have to be very very pretty to make it as an actress these days." I could see that the little girl had completely changed. She got quiet and smaller. You could just tell that her heart was broken. Izzy was fuming like a dragon. I knew she wanted to say something, but she didn't want to create a scene. When they got off the bus Izzy smiled at the girl, her big, dazzling, toothy smile, and maybe it helped a little. I was lucky because whenever I mentioned anything I dreamed of doing I always got to see that smile.

That day Izzy and Anastasia and I got off the bus at the Cathedral of St. John the Divine. There is a statue of a sun and a moon with faces and a man with lots of animals that almost look like they're part of him. Around the big statue there are little statues of animals that school kids made. There are bears, deer and birds. There are also winged horses, a unicorn, a mermaid and a dragon. I believe in those just as much as the others. Because even if nature didn't make them, they exist: in the park next to St. John the Divine.

There are also unicorn tapestries at the Cloisters. The unicorn is my favorite thing about the Cloisters—him and the garden. But both of them are in captivity. The unicorn sits in a field of flowers but there's a fence around him. The herb garden is surrounded by stones. The Cloisters are cold and full of icy marble saints. There are some pretty golden-haired girls—but just their heads—on top of a coffin-type thing and Marys locked in little altars. Izzy and Anastasia hold my hands to keep them warm. They tell me not to be afraid of the scary saints. Izzy says we should come here and dance and hug and kiss to warm it up.

I like St. John the Divine better. There is a chapel dedicated to poets. And one with a giant crystal. There is one for people who died of AIDS. We go there and cry sometimes. We know some of the people whose names are on the altar. At first we only knew a couple, but lately it seems like there are more and more. We go to funerals, for men, mostly—artists, performers, designers—not any older than Izzy or Anastasia. Once we went to one for a baby. The coffin was so little, like for a doll. Anastasia always gives the necklaces she makes out of glass roses to the families of the person who died.

Izzy says, "It's hard to imagine as long as you've been alive this thing has existed."

I say, "Didn't it always?"

"No, Tuck, sweetie," Izzy says. "It's a pretty new thing. Once no one died from having sex. There was no such thing. But someday they will find a cure."

We pray for a cure at the chapel. We pray for Clark and Eddie, who are the adoptive parents of my friend Jasmine—the one I dance with. When I was a little kid I got scared that Jasmine was sick too, but Izzy and Anastasia told me that she was perfectly healthy and that if something bad happened to Clark and Eddie, Jasmine could come live with us. We bring Clark, Eddie and Jasmine groceries and go with them to see *Angels in America* again. Izzy goes to the doctors with Clark and Eddie. Anastasia bakes them lasagnas and pumpkin pies and makes them necklaces out of silver Mexican *milagro* miracle charms to bless them.

Another thing I like about St. John the Divine is the Blessing of the Animals. Once a year everyone brings their animals to get blessed inside the church. There are hundreds and hundreds of dogs. I like how mixed-up-looking dogs are—there are so many different kinds. Besides dogs there are pet birds and rabbits. I even saw a girl holding a white rat. The best part is when the zoo animals come! There is a llama, a pony and a baby elephant with a wrinkly butt. They are so cute with their flowered wreaths being led through the church. There are so many wild-looking creatures in the world. The more wild-looking the better. I wouldn't be surprised to see a unicorn trot up those stairs or a dragon's snakey tail lashing along. There is a two-headed calf in the window of a store on Columbus Avenue. It's stuffed, but it was alive once. People think it's freaky but me, I like it. Because it's different. It has two heads instead of one! It would never be lonely. Izzy says she feels like the two-headed calf sometimes. She doesn't look like it to me. Izzy has only one head unless she is hugging Anastasia. When I am being hugged by Izzy or Anastasia, I am never lonely.

When September came I started junior high at a real school. Up till then I had been having homeschool with Izzy and Anastasia. Izzy taught me math and science and English. Anastasia taught me history and art by underlining stuff in books and taking me to museums. I liked it because they were such good teachers but I thought that I wanted to have more friends my own age, besides Jasmine,

Melody and Phaedra—be like the other kids.

The first day of school Izzy seemed kind of nervous. She took a long time putting on her makeup, and I was scared I was going to be late. She broke a fingernail on the way out the door, and when it happened she looked liked she was going to cry. I wanted to ask her if she would let me take the subway by myself, but she insisted on going with me. I couldn't tell her that I wished she was wearing something a little less flashy, but it would have really made her cry and besides, anything on Izzy looks flashy, with her body and her hair.

Izzy was making me nervous, but I was glad I would get to go to a real school. It went pretty well at first. I was kind of shy, but some kids smiled at me and one girl, Kit, told me she liked my Skechers sneakers.

After school Izzy and Anastasia picked me up. I had been hoping that if they wouldn't let me go home by myself that just one of them would pick me up. I could tell that Kit was looking at us a little funny as we left.

The next day Kit told me that this boy liked me. I felt really shy and weird—I never knew about a boy liking me like that before. She pointed him out.

His name was Alby G. He was wearing a cloth fisherman's hat and had pale-green eyes and a tan. I thought he was cute. I smiled at him with my lips closed so the gap between my front teeth wouldn't show. Alby G. smiled back.

I felt so happy all day. I wanted to dance. My dance would be called "Alby G. Smiled at Me."

But then one day Alby G. he said to me, "Kit says you have two moms."

I go, "Yeah, so?" I thought about the lucky two-headed calf. But it was dead and stuffed.

"You have no dad," Alby G. said.

That was wrong. I knew it was wrong. But I couldn't explain so I ran away.

Alby G. followed me yelling, "Two moms no dad."

He lassoed me with a jump rope and spit in my face. I spit back. I can spit good because of the gap between my two front teeth. All these kids gathered around laughing. Then Izzy came up. Izzy is tall and strong. She was wearing all black, and her red hair was filled with sun like autumn leaves. The kids all ran away. Izzy walked me home.

I was crying by the time we got there.

"Why was Alby G. being mean to you, Tuckling?" Izzy asked.

"He said I had two moms no dad."

"Tuck, I have something to tell you," Izzy said.

And suddenly, I didn't want Izzy to talk. I didn't want her to say another word. I was afraid of what she might tell me. I got up to leave. Izzy asked me to stay. I slumped back. I covered my ears with my hands and started to hum the song Izzy used to sing me for a lullaby: "Blue Moon." Izzy was saying something but I couldn't hear. Izzy touched my arm. She was still talking but I wouldn't listen. Finally she shrugged and tried to kiss me. I pulled away and ran into my room and locked the door.

I knew I had a dad. I wanted to find him. He would be better than any of the other dads. He would wear a suit and go to a real job at an office like the other dads did. He wouldn't be an artist like Anastasia or Izzy. He would shave in the morning but by afternoon his chin would be stubbly again. He would wear round wire-rim glasses. The starchy collar of his white shirt would smell like cigarettes from the cocktail parties he went to but he wouldn't smoke. (I was always trying to get Izzy and Anastasia to stop smoking). He would wear a gold wedding band on his square, strong hand and not false eyelashes or a diamond in his nose. My dad would prefer Jackson Pollock and Mark Rothko to Maxfield Parrish. I think he would look like Calvin Klein. He would pick me up from school, and when the other kids saw me they would never make fun. They would all wish they had a dad like him.

Suddenly I wasn't proud of Anastasia or Izzy anymore. It was more like I was ashamed of them. No other kid at my school lived with two women who slept in the same bed and kissed on the lips all the time. No one else got picked up from school by a six-foot-tall woman in a beaded mini-dress holding hands with a short-haired woman with a pierced nose and leather pants. I wanted a father like everyone else had.

I thought there had to be a clue somewhere. So the next day when I got home from school I started digging around in Anastasia and Izzy's closet. Part of me felt sick to my stomach and wanted to stop. My hands were sweating and my heart was going *thum-thumpety-thump*. It wasn't that I was afraid of getting caught. I was afraid that I might find something I didn't want to see.

I moved aside Izzy's spike heels and Anastasia's boots. I got trapped in the spiderweb of Izzy's lace dress. I sneezed at dusty feather boas. Some of

Izzy's silk roses fell down on my head. Finally I found a box that looked like it might have what I wanted. I opened it up. The box was full of photographs. There were the photo-booth strips that Izzy and Anastasia and I liked to take whenever we went to Coney Island in the summer—all of us freckly, tan, making faces and eating cotton candy. Pictures of us on trips and with our friends Clark and Eddie and Jasmine—some taken before Clark got so thin and Eddie didn't always wear dark glasses. Izzy's glamorous head shots. A picture that this purple-eyed girl had taken of us once, at our Indian restaurant, a few years ago and sent us in the mail. There were pictures of us wearing birthday hats and blowing blowers and eating Anastasia's fat cakes at our birthday parties. At most of the parties it was just me and Izzy and Anastasia. In some Clark and Eddie and Jasmine, and Melody and her mom the performance artist were with us. But that was all. I thought about the kids at school—how they probably had huge birthday parties with everyone from the class bringing them stuff and having fun.

There were no pictures from before I was about two years old. Not even pictures of Izzy or Anastasia. Until I found, at the bottom of the box, a pink book that said "Be My Baby" on the front in gold letters. I opened it up. On the first page was a postcard with a photo of a pink Victorian house. Underneath the postcard it said: "The Pink Gingerbread, San Francisco. Where Tuck was conceived, 1981." I turned the page. There was a really geeky looking picture of me as a baby under the lettering that said, "Baby______ 19__." Someone had written in "Tuck" and 82." On the opposite page the lettering said, "Proud Parents of Baby_______." Someone had written in "Tuck" again, but they had forgotten to put a picture in the space provided. Who was the father whose face should have been in the picture?

I knew I had a father. I knew that once he had stayed at the Pink Gingerbread hotel in San Francisco and that he had made love to my mom there and I had been conceived. I knew that his face belonged on the empty page.

So I decided to find him.

I stole the cash from inside the Victorian lace-up boot that Izzy got at a thrift store once. It was Izzy's emergency money—tips from her cocktail waitress job. This was an emergency. I bought a plane ticket. I put some clothes in a bag and took a cab to J.F.K. the way I'd done with Izzy and Anastasia when we went to London last summer. Part of me was scared, but when I found my dad I wanted him to know how brave I was.

At the airport scary-looking men tried to get me into cars with them but I just ignored them and ran to the terminal and got on the plane to San Francisco. The stewardess kept asking me if I needed another barf bag thing because she said I looked so pale. Even with all the loud noises and grumpy people and the scary men and the fakey stewardess with her barf bags, the trip wasn't hard. Izzy and Anastasia had taught me that I was strong enough to do anything I wanted, if I wanted it bad enough. And I wanted my father bad enough. But I didn't tell Izzy and Anastasia where I was going. Knowing them they probably would have wanted to go with me and help me find him. They would have wanted me to tell them all my feelings. Maybe they would have taken me with them to see their shrink, who reminded me of Woody Allen when we ran into him at *Angels in America* once. But I was suddenly too mad at Izzy and Anastasia to tell them anything. I was sick of how they always tried to understand and explain everything. I wanted a nice quiet father who would just take care of what was wrong in a calm, efficient way. Without tears and sharing and making everyone tell all their secrets.

I wanted a father who didn't see a shrink, who didn't dress up in crazy clothes and perform in stage shows, who didn't work at a bar, whose best friends weren't dying from AIDS. Maybe someone at the Pink Gingerbread would know where I could find him.

San Francisco

I flew into San Francisco in the afternoon. It was a clear, warm, windy day. The light was blue and sparkly, almost sapphire. I told the cab driver that I wanted to go to the Pink Gingerbread. I probably talked really loud because my ears still hadn't popped from the plane ride, even though I'd been chewing gum the whole way. The gum had made my mouth stale-tasting and dry. I had a headache from the light that was much harsher than the light in Manhattan, even on a bright day there.

The driver got on the highway from where you could see the hills of the city covered with pastel houses. We got off and drove up and down scary roller-coaster streets past Victorian homes and cable cars and little stores selling produce, Italian food, books, liquor, tobacco, coffee, occult supplies. I saw some punks with orange and purple hair, a barefoot girl in a black-velvet dress dancing down the street, some men with red eyes sitting on a porch, a boy with a huge top hat riding a unicycle, a group of cute giggling Japanese schoolgirls in short skirts and platform shoes.

There was no problem guessing which building was the Pink Gingerbread. It was painted bright pink and covered with fancy carvings and curlicues. I thought, This is where my dad and mom made me, in this cake-house, in this city with the light like a blue gem. They probably ate fettuccine first, or Chinese noodles. They probably kissed in a cable car and walked up hills so steep that their calves ached.

I went inside the Pink Gingerbread. A large woman in a tie-dyed caftan was sitting at a desk with blue and green glass beads hanging all around her.

"Hello and welcome to the Pink Ginger," she said.

"Hi," I said. "I'd like a room."

"Are you alone?" she asked.

I nodded, hoping she wouldn't freak.

"No one's ever really alone here," she said. "I'll help you with anything you need. Now, which room would you like? There's the Venus room, the Buddha room, the Jimi Hendrix room, the Janis Joplin room, the John and Yoko . . ."

"I want that one," I said. Then I wondered why I had chosen it. After all, I was trying to get away from Izzy and Anastasia, not be reminded of them. I wanted my father. The way I'd imagined him, he probably wouldn't have chosen the John and Yoko room; he probably wouldn't even have stayed here at all. But I was used to living with Izzy and Anastasia. And I felt stupid changing my mind. I paid for the room.

"Well, come with me," the woman said.

I followed her upstairs and down a hallway.

"I'm Mellow Moon," she said. "I've run this place for thirty years."

"Wow," I said. But I wasn't that impressed. Except that maybe she was here when my dad came. I wanted to ask about him but I decided to wait. Mellow Moon opened a door. Inside, the room was decorated with a huge mural of John and Yoko. There was a low white bed like the one they did their bed-in in. There was a jar of daisies and a bowl full of acorns like the ones from John and Yoko's art project where they had all the world leaders plant trees for peace. Izzy and Anastasia and I planted a tree in Central Park for peace once.

"Breakfast comes with," Mellow Moon said. "We serve from eight till eleven. There's a map if you want. Just ring down if you need anything else." And she left.

I was kind of tired from traveling and my ears hurt—they still hadn't popped. My mouth still tasted of old chewing gum. I tried not to think about Izzy and Anastasia and how they were doing their day, not knowing that I was gone. I tried not to think about how, whenever we got to a hotel, Izzy pulled the bedspread off, first thing, because they grossed her out, and asked for extra towels, and how Anastasia opened the windows and lit the incense she brought.

So I wouldn't get lonely, I decided I'd check out the city, see a little of what my parents saw.

Golden Gate Park was pretty close to the hotel so I walked there. On the way I saw punks and hippies and art students and homeless people hanging out, skateboarding, drinking coffee, eating burritos. There was a certain sad kind of feeling that I didn't feel in New York. Maybe because in New York everyone moves so fast they don't have time to think about the sadness. Maybe because San Francisco is so pretty that in contrast to the pastry houses and colorful clothes and sparkling blueness, the faces look more sad. Maybe because of how I was feeling, but I didn't want to think it was that.

I walked into the park. It was different from Central Park, where you sort of always know you are in a place someone made specially in the middle of a city so everyone wouldn't go completely crazy. Central Park feels like it was made after the city existed, instead of like all the land was that way once. But Golden Gate Park feels like fairyland and like the fairies said it was okay to build the rest of San Francisco around it, as long as the park got to stay the way it was. You can walk just a little ways and be all alone, surrounded by flowers of every color (Izzy would think she was in paradise) or in the best-smelling herb garden (Anastasia would get inspired to cook some new dish). Then suddenly you find another surprise. I found two stone statues of creatures with men's heads, women's breasts and lions' butts. They were a little scary. I found a carousel with all kinds of real and mythical beasts on it—deer, giraffe, ostrich, frog, wildcat and a unicorn, a dragon. I found a Japanese garden where I drank green tea and ate sweet-and-salty crunchy tidbits served by ladies in kimonos. There was a giant Buddha statue, a little red temple called a spirit house, shallow pools full of carp and irises and wish-pennies and a steep red-lacquer bridge. I climbed up on the bridge, closed my eyes, tossed a penny over my shoulder and wished. I want to find my dad, I wished. Then I left there and found a botanical garden with rhododendrons and a duck pond, willow trees, white flowers like bells, fern grottoes, a Mexican cloud forest, and a redwood forest with benches dedicated to people who had died. After a while it started to get dark and my legs were getting tired and all the beauty of the park felt like too much, almost sinister, like at night suddenly the slippery water fairies would slither out of the pools with their long grasping fingers and the scaly tree fairies would jump out of the trees with their sharp teeth and the stone sphinxes would start hissing and there wouldn't be any fathers who didn't believe in fairies or sphinxes to protect me by saying, "That's all just your imagination, Tuck. Let's go get a nice big steak for dinner."

That thought made me hungry, but Izzy and

Anastasia never ate steak, so I couldn't really imagine eating one. Instead I stopped at a Middle Eastern restaurant on the way home. I sat on some cushions on the floor next to a hippie couple smoking a hookah pipe, and I ordered baba ganoush and pita bread and grape leaves. I'd have to wait for the steak until I found my dad.

When I got back to the Pink Gingerbread I started to worry. I thought about Izzy and Anastasia and how they were probably crying and freaking out and calling the police by now. I didn't want to make them so scared, but I couldn't call them yet. I would soon, I promised myself. As soon as I had a clue. Because if I called them they'd get me to say where I was and they'd come and get me and want to have this big pow-wow thing and I just couldn't handle it. So I took a bath in the tub down the hall and I put on a clean T-shirt and got into the huge white John-and-Yoko bed. I closed my eyes and thought about my mom and dad lying maybe in this very same room after a day of stuffing themselves with art and croissants and coffee, a day of steep hills and cable cars and sapphire light and carousels and kissing, and how they might have laid down on this very bed and imagined what I'd be like. I was pretty sure that they knew they were trying to have me when they did. I was pretty sure I was wanted. But then where was my dad now? I wondered. If he had wanted me then, where was he now?

I woke up and put on some of my big jeans and my Skechers and went downstairs to the dining room. There were a few oak tables and chairs and a buffet of fresh strawberries, melons, peaches and oranges, blueberry muffins, bagels, cream cheese, juice, coffee and Celestial Seasonings teas. I took three strawberries, a muffin and some juice and sat down. I was the only one there. Then I noticed something. There was a bookshelf with lots of big notebooks on it. I went over and picked one up. It said: "Pink Gingerbread Guest Book, December 1994–June 1995." I put it down and picked up another. It said the same thing except the dates were from 1989. There were lots of these books. I remembered the postcard in my baby book. 1981. If I could find the guest book for that year I might be able to find my parents' names!

"Mellow Moon!" I called. "Mellow Moon!" There was no answer. I called her name again. I figured she must be around here somewhere. Someone had put out the food.

Then Mellow Moon came in wearing a caftan printed with moon faces and stars. She looked bright and beaming. "Good morning, lovely," she said. "Sleep well?"

"Mellow Moon," I said, "Do you have guest books going back to 1981?" I thought for a moment, counting. I was born in May, 1982. So the date I was looking for was . . . "August, 1981," I said.

"Oh yes," said Mellow Moon. "Let me see."

She knelt down and looked through some note-books. I sat next to her and looked too. Finally she said, "Here we go!" and handed me the book. I opened it up and started looking through all the signatures. They were written in bright crayon. Some people had done psychedelic drawings too. Most of them had written their addresses.

"Looking for someone?" Mellow Moon said, smiling all round and peaceful like her name.

"Yep," I said. "But I don't know their names. I just know they stayed here then."

"Then how will you know who they are?" Mellow Moon asked.

"I just will, I think," I said. "At least I hope." I turned the pages slowly, carefully reading each name, thinking that maybe one of them would seem right. Izzy has always told me she does everything by intuition.

"It's the only way," she says. "Just feel it."

I held my hand over each name, feeling for some kind of buzz, some kind of sign, maybe. Nothing nothing nothing. Just a bunch of names. Until I saw a name I knew, "Anastasia."

"Anastasia!" I said.

"I thought you didn't know the name," said Mellow Moon.

It was hard to explain to her. I knew then that Anastasia was my real mom. That didn't surprise me. But next to her name was another one—a man's name! "Irving Rose."

"Irving Rose?" I said. It wasn't what I'd imagined. I'd imagined something more like Calvin or Clay or Griffin. Oh well.

"Irving Rose," Mellow Moon repeated. "Do you know, I think I remember him, believe it or not."

"No way!" I said. "Tell me, Mellow Moon, what do you remember?" Was he serious but kind? I wanted to ask. Mentally stable? Shrink-less? Handsome? Did he wear Armani suits and wire rims?

But Mellow Moon said, "I remember him because of his hair, which was beautiful red like yours and because it went with his name: Rose. And I remember that he was very warm to me, very funny. He dressed up in a giant sun costume one morning to surprise me, and he sang, 'You are my moonshine' to me at breakfast. The hotel was full then—it was summer—and everyone sat around laughing. They all loved him. He was a beautiful man," said Mellow Moon.

I looked at the guest book and read:

Dear Mellow Moon:

Thank you for your hospitality. What a romantic place the Pink Ginger is! We have chosen it specially as the place where our child will be conceived. The John and Yoko room seems like the perfect environment. Last night we took cable cars through the city, ate noodles in an underground restaurant in Chinatown that used to be an opium den, went to the museum, walked some more and ate pasta in North Beach at a restaurant with a miniature replica of the Trevi fountain. Then we walked back to the Pink Ginger and our beautiful room. In the morning we enjoyed your sumptuous buffet and then walked to the park. We especially loved the Japanese tea garden, the rose garden, the botanical gardens and the carousel. We returned to eat baba ganoush and pita bread and stuffed grape leaves sitting on cushions on the floor of the Middle Eastern place down the street, then went back to our room again. Maybe we'll come back here with our child some day. If you are ever in L.A. look us up!

Love,
Irving and Anastasia Rose

Then came the best part of all: their address in L.A. I couldn't believe it. He wasn't the way I'd imagined him, but I had to admit I was starting to like this Irving Rose, even though his name was kind of goofy-sounding.

I felt like doing a dance, right there in the Pink Ginger. The dance would be called "I Was Made at a Hippie Hotel."

"Are you going to stay here another night?" asked Mellow Moon.

"No," I said. "I can't. I have business." I wrote down the address from the guest book.

I went upstairs to grab my stuff, and then I paid Mellow Moon for the night in the John and Yoko room. "Is there anything else you remember about Irving Rose?" I asked her.

"I remember thinking," said Mellow Moon, "that he was going to make the best father I'd ever seen. We were talking about having children. He wanted a child so much. I said that I never did because my parents disappointed me even though they tried to love me as best they could and I didn't want my children to resent me the way I couldn't help resenting my parents. But Irving Rose didn't care. He said he would try not to disappoint his child, but that even if he did he would continue to love her and hope that she could love him."

"Thank you, Mellow Moon," I said. I started to leave, but she put her big soft caftan arms around me and gave me a hug. Because I had been thinking about being hugged by the strong, hard, muscular, suited arms of my lost father, Mellow Moon's hug bugged me a little, but it also felt good. I had grown up used to having double-mama hugs every day of my life and the last day was the first time I hadn't had even one.

"Good-bye, Moon," I said, thinking about the kids' book that Izzy liked to read out loud to us.

"Good-bye, little Tuck."

Los Angeles

I took the Green Tortoise Bus to L.A. It was pretty boring. Most people slept or read. There wasn't much to look at out the window except some dusty oleander bushes, some fields, a few grazing cows, cars and a weird whitish sky. I was getting lonely. Whenever I rode on buses or subways with Izzy and Anastasia we sang or talked about the play or exhibit we had just seen, the meal we were going to have. Sometimes we made up stories about the lives of the other people on board, but we had to do that pretty quietly. Once we were making up a story about this man with a big scar on his cheek, how we thought he was a hit man, and I think he heard us. He followed us for three blocks when we got off the bus. It was scary then, but while I was riding to L.A. I even missed getting into trouble with Izzy and Anastasia. By now they were probably out of their minds with worry. But I figured I could find my dad really fast and then as soon as I did I'd call them. Hopefully it would be before my name and picture appeared on any milk cartons or in the post office. Just in case anyone might recognize me I was wearing a hooded sweatshirt and a pair of tiny round sunglasses that I'd bought on the street in San Francisco. I kept thinking about my dad and wondering what he would think of me trying to find him like this. I imagined that he wouldn't like it. He was a careful kind of person who would worry about me being out on my own. He would scold me. But deep down inside he would be proud of how brave and determined I am.

When I arrived in Hollywood, my legs were stiff and I was hungry. Nothing looked the way I had imagined it. There were stars on the pavement, but they were covered with old wads of chewing gum and layers of grimy dirt. The people didn't look like stars either. There were street kids as pale as New Yorkers and homeless people with shopping carts full of stuff and prostitutes with bad skin under too much makeup. The most glamorous thing about it was the cars. They looked big and expensive and they were everywhere. Also, the billboards had giant pictures of sexy people with pouty lips in underwear and there was a mural of Charlie Chaplin and Humphrey Bogart and Marilyn Monroe and James Dean and Shirley Temple sitting in a movie theater. Oh, and the movie theaters themselves looked pretty cool still. Especially the Chinese, like a red-lacquer pagoda with the hand and foot prints in the cement in front. It was weird to see how tiny all the women's feet looked in their spike heels. Betty Grable's whole leg print was an especially popular attraction for the tourists, who seemed like they were from Japan and maybe Germany mostly. If Izzy were here, I thought, she'd probably embarrass me by lying down in Betty Grable's leg print and saying, "That girl had the littlest legs I've ever seen! Come here, Tuck, you try!" I thought about seeing a movie and getting something to eat, but I knew I should save my money and my time, so I bought a map and asked the guy at the souvenir store how to get to the street that Irving Rose had written down in the Pink Ginger guest book.

It wasn't too far away from Hollywood Boulevard. The street was lined with palm trees and tiny bungalow-style houses with overgrown gardens. It seemed weird to me how many flowers were everywhere. Even though the air was hot and smoggy and there was something hardish about the city, the flowers looked brave and in-your-face—almost demented, though, in a way, like the hard work was getting to them.

The address I wanted was a building that looked like a group of tiny Swiss chateaux with a garden full of lemon and orange trees, some ragged roses, spiky purple agapanthus and fluffy pastel puffs of hydrangea. (Izzy taught me the names agapanthus and hydrangea because she thought they were so weird for such pretty things). When they saw me, two gray doves flew out of a mossy birdbath and onto a wall, flashing the white fans of their tails. The wall was covered with passionflower vines—passionflowers like weird sea creatures that would close up around your fingers if you touched them, and bright-orange, bursting passionflower fruits. There was a garden path made of stones winding among the apartments. The one I came to had the best rosebush in the place and a stone frog family sitting in front. I thought about the fairy tale where the girl kisses the frog to get a prince. Too bad you can't get fathers that way, I thought. The passionflower vines had almost covered the whole apartment, except for the door. It was a little hard to imagine my imagined father living here, but I liked it anyway.

I knocked and waited. I knocked again. My heart was imitating my fist. What if my father answered the door? After a while I heard footsteps and the sound of a peephole opening. A tall white-haired man, with a huge white moustache that curled up at the ends, opened the door.

"Hello," he boomed Swissly.

"Hi," I said. "I'm looking for somebody."

"Who are you looking for?" He twirled the end of his moustache around his finger and glowered at me.

"Irving Rose," I said.

The man's blue eyes looked like they were doing a jig and the rest of his body seemed like it would follow any second. His cheeks turned pinker. "You know Irving Rose! The genius! I haven't seen him in years."

"He used to live here?" I asked.

"Yes he did. In this very apartment. I moved in when he left."

"Who are you?" I asked.

"The landlord, Uncle Hansel," the man said. He

bowed so low that I was afraid his moustache would tickle me. Instead all that happened was I got a little dizzy from his cologne. Then he put out his big hand and I shook it. I tried to see behind him, into the apartment where my father used to live.

"Could I come in?" I asked.

"Didn't anyone tell you that children shouldn't go into the apartments of strange men!" Uncle Hansel scolded.

"You're not strange," I reassured him, still trying to see.

"Well, all right, but we'll leave the door wide open and you must run out if you feel in the least uncomfortable, dear," Uncle Hansel insisted.

I followed him to a small, dim room that smelled of rye bread and strawberry jam. It was filled with wooden furniture carved and painted with hearts and flowers. There were jars of roses, ferns in bird-cages, a collection of mechanical windup toys and as many cuckoo clocks as could fit on the walls. As I looked at them, they all started chiming, and a flock of wooden cuckoos scooted in and out. I wondered if that drove Uncle Hansel crazy, but he seemed to be enjoying it. He smiled proudly at the birds and twirled his moustache.

"Would you like something to eat?" Uncle Hansel asked. "Although, come to think of it, little girls aren't supposed to accept food from strangers."

"You knew my father, though," I said. I was hungry, and I had a pretty good sense of smell—I bet there really would be rye bread and jam.

"Your father!" Uncle Hansel exclaimed. "Why of course! The genius! You look just like him!"

"So could I maybe have a snack?" I asked.

"Of course. Come with me."

I followed him into the tiny kitchen. There were more cuckoos on the walls, and plates painted with flowers, fruits and country landscapes. Uncle Hansel pulled back a wooden chair painted with a design of red hearts and apples and little green leaves and vines. I sat down. He opened the oven and took out a round bread with a shiny golden crust. I was right—rye. When he cut it open, steam rose up. He put a slice on a plate and set it down in front of me with some strawberry jam. (Right again!) Then Hansel got a jar of canned herrings out of the refrigerator and put some water on to boil. He sat beside me, speared a herring and held it up in front of my face. I shook my head.

"Jam is great," I said.

He shrugged, plopped the herring onto his bread

and slid it all into his mouth. He wiped his moustache, sat back and smiled, hands resting on his belly, while I ate my bread and jam.

"Can you tell me about Irving Rose?" I said after I had finished eating and we were sipping tea from cups so small that I was afraid he would crush them with his big hands. It had been hard to wait, but I didn't want to seem too eagerish.

"The genius!" Uncle Hansel said. "What a delight!"

"How well did you now him?"

Uncle Hansel was thinking. I could tell by the way he touched his moustache. "Everyone felt as if he knew *them* well," Uncle Hansel said. "You just felt so comfortable with the man. But when you thought about him later, after he'd left, you felt as if you didn't know him much at all. He was a bit mysterious in that way. But I believe that's how geniuses are. Now, I'm not one myself as I'm sure you can see, but that one was. So you probably are as well . . . what shall I call you?"

"Tuck," I said. I almost said Tuckling. I hadn't heard anyone use that name in months, it felt like.

"Tuck the little genius!" Uncle Hansel said. He had a tone in his voice that made me scared he would reach over and pinch my cheeks or something.

"What else do you remember about him?" I asked, hoping he wouldn't pinch me.

"Well, he liked to dress up. He dressed up as a cuckoo clock once. He wore a big clock with a door for his face and stuck out his head with a bird mask on and made cuckoo sounds. And he loved his wife. Anna. They loved each other with all their hearts, you could see that. And he always wanted everyone to smile. He wanted you to believe in yourself."

"His wife, Anastasia?" I said.

"Yes, I think so. Anastasia. Anna. She was very quiet. A good cook. Though a bit eccentric with her recipes."

"She's my mother," I said. "I live with her. But I'm looking for my father."

"Then they aren't together anymore?" Uncle Hansel said. "How sad. I'm surprised. They were best friends besides being in love."

He wound up a plastic Woodstock and set it down on the table. It hopped around. I was afraid it would hop off, but it didn't. It didn't stop hopping either. Finally I started wishing it would fall.

"Do you know how I can find him?" I asked.

Uncle Hansel twirled his moustache and

watched the Woodstock hop around. "Actually he did leave a forwarding address. His parents' home I believe. I liked him so much that I wanted to keep in touch, but we never really did. Let me see."

He got up. Woodstock stopped, but then a plastic Charlie Chaplin started waddling around. It must have been in Uncle Hansel's pocket because I hadn't seen it before. I wanted to push it off the table. My nerves felt like windup toys. It felt like I was waiting—watching that Charlie waddle around—forever.

Finally Uncle Hansel came back. "Did I tell you that these apartments were built by Charlie Chaplin?" he asked, watching the windup Charlie.

"Did you find anything?" I asked.

"Oh yes! Here we are," Uncle Hansel trumpeted triumphantly. He copied something out of a phone book and handed it to me. It said: *Irving Rose c/o Molly and Herby Rose.* Then there was an address in Sherman Oaks, California.

"Where's that?" I asked. I wanted to do a dance. My dance would be called "Finding Father: Uncle Hansel Helps."

"Are you planning to go to Sherman Oaks?" Uncle Hansel asked.

"I want to find my father," I said. "Is it far?"

"How far have you come already?" Hansel asked.

"From Manhattan."

"Then this isn't far at all. I can drive you, if you like. Although, as a rule you really shouldn't get into cars with people unless you know them very well. But I did know your dear father and mother and served you my home-baked rye bread in my own home, so I suppose we can make an exception this time."

"That would be so cool," I said. "Thank you, Uncle Hansel. Can we go now?"

"I don't see why not. But does your mother, Anna, know where you are? She must be terribly worried."

"She knows," I lied. "I told her I was going to go looking for my father."

"You seem a little young to be out on your own."

"I'm very self-sufficient," I said.

"Well, all right."

The Charlie Chaplin stopped waddling. Before I could sigh with relief the Woodstock started hopping again.

It was still hopping when Uncle Hansel and I left the apartment and got into his boatish car. He drove me through the hot smoggy city, over the canyon filled with houses that looked as if they were growing out of the hill, beside yucca plants like white torches and other flowers with funny names, into the hotter smoggier valley.

I heard the carousel tinkle of an ice-cream truck. I smelled citrus and smog. I saw houses with lawns and basketball nets over the garage and lots of shiny cars. I saw people with tans.

I missed Manhattan. I missed the pretzels stale on the street and crystaled with salt. I missed pasty-faced people rushing to their shrink appointments or their offices or the theater. I even missed the sound of sirens that always got recorded on our answering machine announcement. I missed sitting on the steps of the Met and watching the people drugged on art. I missed the angel in the park watching over all of us. I missed unicorns. I missed being called Tuckling. I missed guessing what herbs were in the dinner and listening to bedtime stories in front of the fireplace. I missed . . . I missed Anastasia. I missed Izzy. Nothing made sense all of a sudden.

"Are you all right, my dear?" Uncle Hansel asked. "You're awfully quiet. Are you sure your mother knows where you are?"

But luckily I didn't have to answer him because I recognized the name of the street where Molly and Herby Rose lived, and I pointed it out to Hansel, and he turned the car and stopped in front of a pale-yellow house with green shutters and insane-looking gargantuan roses growing in front of it.

"Thank you, Uncle Hansel," I said.

"Don't you want me to go in with you?" he asked. "What if your grandparents don't live there anymore?"

"I'm sure I'll be fine," I said.

I said good-bye to him and got out of the car. Then I went up the path past the pink, yellow, peach and red roses to the green door. I felt dizzy from the smell of the roses and the heat and smog. I felt like a windup toy. I half expected a cuckoo bird to stick its head out of the door when I rang the bell.

A little old red-haired lady, not much taller than me, opened the door. As soon as I saw her gap-toothed grin, I knew I was in the right place. I looked back at Uncle Hansel and waved. He stuck his head out of the car, squinted at the lady and waved back. Then he drove away. I hoped that the Woodstock had stopped hopping by the time he got home. Or maybe he'd like it to still be pecking around.

The lady asked me my name.

"Tuck," I said. "I think I'm your granddaughter."

This made her grin get even bigger. "My granddaughter!" she giggled giddily. "Come in!"

I went into the house with her. It was sunny and clean. There were books stacked everywhere and Chagall prints on the walls, some Cubist paintings and a poster of Albert Einstein with his tongue sticking out. Mobiles hung from the ceiling. I could hear someone playing the violin in the next room.

"Just a moment," the lady said. "Sit down and make yourself at home. I'll be right back, *bubela*."

She walked on tiptoe out of the room. The violin music stopped. I heard soft voices. She came back holding the hand of a sad-looking old man.

"This is our granddaughter, *bubela*," the woman said.

I wasn't sure if she were calling him *bubela* or if she thought that was my name. "Tuck," I said. I shook the man's hand, which still seemed to vibrate, maybe from playing the violin. He looked at me with his sad eyes and smiled shyly.

"Then you know where . . . does this mean . . ."

"He is wondering about your father," the woman said. "We haven't seen your father in years and years. He only writes to us at the high holidays with no return address. We don't know anything about him anymore."

My heart tumbled down a staircase inside of me like a broken windup Woodstock. "I came here looking for him," I said.

"So you don't know about Irving either?" the man sighed.

I shook my head. "I never knew him. I found your address and thought you'd know where he is."

"What a shame!" the woman said. "We love him so much. Why doesn't he want to see us anymore?"

I didn't know what to say to her. I watched the abstract shapes on a mobile move in the breeze that came rosily through one of the open windows. I suddenly felt so tired.

"But the important thing now," the woman said, "is that Tuck is here with us. Isn't that a blessing, Herby? Tuck is here! Our granddaughter. And she is so beautiful, isn't she?"

I was afraid she might pinch my cheeks.

Herby smiled sadly and nodded. "She looks just like you, Molly," he said.

Nobody except Izzy and Anastasia had ever said I was beautiful before. I guess that's what grandparents say. But it seemed like they meant it. I had to admit I did look like my grandmother, anyway.

Even though I was sad about them not knowing where my dad was, I was glad that I'd found them. They showed me their art books and mobiles and rose garden. Molly served a noodle kugel made with cinnamon and apples. We ate at a yellow Formica table in the kitchen. Herby played his violin for me, and it made tears pop into my eyes even though I tried to hide them. He and Molly reminded me of people in a Chagall painting. I could just imagine them when they were younger holding hands and flying around upside down with their roses all around them.

"Would you like to see Irving's room?" Molly asked.

And so I followed her and Herby down the hallway and into a bedroom that looked as if no one had rearranged it for years.

It wasn't the room I would have imagined my dream-father growing up in. That room would have had parchment maps on the walls, glow-in-the-dark constellations pasted on the ceiling, books about astronauts and dinosaurs. This room had posters of Andy Warhol, Edie Sedgewick, Marilyn Monroe,

Jimi Hendrix, the Beatles, Iggy Pop, Marlene Dietrich, Patti Smith by Robert Mapplethorpe, David Bowie as Ziggy Stardust. It had a purple-velveteen bedspread on the bed and a piece of tie-dyed fabric on the ceiling. There was one of those mirrored disco ball things too. It wasn't what I'd imagined but I liked it. I wanted to hang out here. I wanted to dress up like David Bowie and turn on the disco ball and dance. The dance would be called "My Dad as a Teen."

"You could stay here if you want," Molly said. "We keep it just like he left it. Cleaner of course. We miss him so much."

"Can you stay?" Herby asked. His voice was deep but so soft it was hard to hear him. I could tell he was still thinking about Irving.

"Thanks; okay," I said.

I stayed that night in my father's boy bed. I thought I'd probably dream about him, but instead I dreamed about Izzy and Anastasia. Izzy was playing the violin. She and Anastasia were flying around in a rose garden in the clouds like out of a Chagall painting. They were flying over the Pink Gingerbread. Izzy was sticking out her tongue at a billboard with Albert Einstein on it. Anastasia had a mobile on top of her beanie hat. Izzy was wearing her lace-up Victorian boots. There were thousands of plastic Victorian-boot windup toys hopping around in my dream. I felt so bad because each one reminded me of the money I'd stolen out of Izzy's.

It was a weird dream. It made me miss Izzy and Anastasia a lot. Herby and Molly were nice. Everyone had been nice—Mellow Moon and Uncle Hansel—but I wanted to be home. I hadn't found what I'd wanted, so I just wanted to go home.

I told Herby and Molly over breakfast bagels that I had to get back to New York. Herby looked sadder than usual, and Molly reached over to pinch my cheeks. I let her.

"Well, you be in touch with us, Tuck," she said. "You call us any time and visit any time. And if you ever see your father, tell him to call us. Tell him that whatever lifestyle he has chosen for himself, we will always love him."

I gave them my address in Manhattan. They insisted on going with me to the airport and buying me a ticket back to New York. I wished that they could come back with me. Izzy and Anastasia would have liked them, I thought. But it might have been hard for Molly and Herby to handle—two women kissing and sleeping in the same bed and everything.

When the plane took off, I got the envelope Molly had given me out of my backpack. She had handed it to me just before I got on the plane.

"Irving didn't like his picture taken," Molly had said. "Even when he was a little boy. He always skipped school on picture day. But I managed to take this one, when he was sixteen. It's the only one, but I want you to have it."

I'd decided to wait until I was flying to open the envelope. Otherwise I was afraid I wouldn't be able to leave. I'd want to just stay locked up in my dad's childhood room, looking at his picture for the rest of my life like some creepy psycho.

I ran my finger along under the flap of the envelope. I tore it. I opened it. I closed my eyes and took out what was inside.

I opened my eyes to look at the picture of . . .

Of course. How could I have been so dumb? Who else had red hair and the warmest gap-toothed smile? Who else was beautiful and made everyone feel happy? Izzy. Izzy Budd was Irving Rose. Irving Rose was Izzy Budd. At sixteen Izzy was a tall thin boy with shaggy red hair hanging in his eyes. He looked awkward and shy but he was grinning like he thought it would make the person taking the picture feel better. Izzy was not just my second mama.

Izzy was my father.

Manhattan

When I got back to the apartment Izzy and Anastasia were both there, sitting on the floor smoking cigarettes, which is something they never did inside. The whole place smelled of smoke. They looked like they were wearing white face powder and had each lost weight. Neither of them had on any of Anastasia's jewelry. Izzy was dressed differently than I had ever seen her in a white men's T-shirt and black trousers. Her hair was slicked back from her face and she didn't have any makeup on. When they saw me, they crunched out their cigarettes and both just started to cry.

I put my arms around them and held on like they were parts of my body that I had lost for a while. I thought about the two-headed calf.

"I'm so sorry," I said. "I'm so sorry I made you worry. I was looking for my father."

"Oh honey, Tuck, I tried to tell you," Izzy said. "Why didn't you listen?"

"I was scared," I said. "I had to find it out myself."

"Do you want to know more?" Izzy asked in a soft, hoarse voice. I used to think the word hoarse came from the sound of little horses in your throat and that was what it sounded like now.

"Okay," I said.

This is the story Izzy told me about how I was born.

Irving Rose had known for as long as he could remember that he wanted to be a girl. It was as if this girl was living inside of him, waiting. The kids at school knew. They teased him all the time. "Is Irving or isn't he?" they sang. "Is he or isn't he?" That was how he got the name Izzy.

Irving studied hard, got perfect grades. He was alone a lot growing up. The biggest problem was that even though Irving felt like a girl inside, he didn't love boys. He knew there were some boys in his school who loved boys and he wished he were like them. It would have made everything a little less complicated, maybe. He thought that his parents might be able to understand if one day he went to them and told them he was gay. They would have been able to read about it, or ask their psychiatrist friends. But what Irving felt was different from that. He didn't even know what to call it. He wanted to be a girl and he wanted to love girls. He admired them from afar, but he was as afraid of them as he was of the boys who teased him. The girl he liked the most was tan and thin with brown hair that looked as if she had cut it herself and stuck back with kids' plastic barrettes. Irving thought she looked good even in her ugly gym shorts and striped acrylic T-shirt. She always wore lots of jewelry—silver hoops in her ears, colorful glass beads, armloads of bracelets and a ring that looked like a real eye encased in glass. She got suspended from school for wearing boys' boxer shorts under her gym shorts and for smoking in the girls' room. Her laugh was scratchy and made his spine tingle. He had only heard her laugh a few times, mostly when her best friend, who had long hair and big breasts, whispered things in her ear. Irving watched this girl for years and never spoke to her. Her name was Ann.

Senior year of high school, Ann's best friend moved away. Ann never laughed or wore jewelry anymore. She was at school every day. Her tan peeled off. She always looked as if she had been crying. Irving went up to Ann and asked her if she'd like to go to get a pizza with him. She shrugged and said okay.

It was the best day of Irving's life. He borrowed his mom's Volvo station wagon and picked Ann up. They went out for pizza and then they drove around the valley. Irving hardly noticed all the things he hated about where he lived—the smog and heat and mini-malls, the people all trying to look the same. He hardly thought about how much he wanted to move to Hollywood or San Francisco or Manhattan. All he thought about was Ann sitting beside him, playing with her eye-ring, the first piece of jewelry Irving had seen her wear since her friend left. It was on Ann's middle finger.

"Tell me about your ring," Irving said.

Ann looked into his sad eyes and said, "I'm gay." She told him about how, when her girlfriend's parents found out, they'd moved away and forbidden their daughter to ever speak or write to Ann again. Ann started to cry. Irving pulled the car over at the side of the road under some eucalyptus trees and sat quietly while she cried, trying to put his thoughts around her like arms. When she had stopped crying, Ann asked Irving to tell her something about himself. Irving told Ann that he wanted to be a woman and that he was in love with her. It all seemed so simple and right, somehow, when he told Ann. It was the first time he had said it out loud, or even let himself think it all the way through.

Ann didn't look shocked or angry or even surprised. She said it was a lot to think about and asked Irving to take her home. When they got to her house she took off the eye-ring and gave it to Irving. Then she kissed his cheek and went inside.

The next day Irving asked Ann to go out with him again. When she came out to meet him, wearing all her silver jewelry and glass beads, she saw, in the driver's seat of the Volvo, a beautiful woman with long curly red hair.

"I'm Izzy," the woman said. "Irving couldn't make it."

Ann smiled. "You're beautiful, Izzy," she said.

"Thank you, honey." Izzy smiled. "And tell me your name."

Ann thought about it. She had always hated Ann. It never felt exotic enough. She looked at Izzy in her high heels and lipstick, being exactly who she wanted to be. "Anastasia," Ann said.

"I feel like a dragon, Anastasia," Izzy said. "Freaky and angry."

"Dragons are sacred and powerful," said Anastasia. "Let's move to Manhattan where they surround the Dakota and breathe up through the grates in the sidewalk. You'll feel at home there."

"Dragons in Manhattan," Izzy said. "I like that."

That night they realized that they would love each other for the rest of their lives, no matter what they had to go through. They never touched each other as lovers for years, even after they had moved out of their parents' houses and over the hill into a faux-Swiss-chateau apartment that had been built by Charlie Chaplin. Anastasia dyed her hair black and pierced her nose. Irving began to grow his hair long. He got a job as a waiter, and Anastasia studied at the Fashion Insititute and sold her jewelry to make money. Irving dressed up as Izzy and modeled it. Anastasia and her mysterious model became wildly popular and made a lot of money, most of which they saved. A while later, they took a trip to the Pink Gingerbread in San Francisco and Irving made love to Anastasia for the first and only time as Irving, so that they could have a baby. After that they went to Europe and Irving had the operation and became Izzy. Izzy believed that she could never see her parents, Herby and Molly again. All she could do was send them cards on holidays. She missed them very much—her father with his violin, her mother with her roses, like people in a Chagall.

But Izzy finally had her true body. And she had Anastasia. Even though, ever since the change, Anastasia had grown quieter and quieter, as if she were afraid of letting out Izzy's secret if she spoke.

Izzy and Anastasia moved to Manhattan where dragons live and Anastasia gave birth to a baby girl. Izzy felt as if she had carried the baby too, as if she had gone through the labor along with Anastasia. Izzy thought that instead of giving their child one of their last names, they should create a new one for all of them. Anastasia, who had become even quieter, afraid of giving away the secret to the baby, wrote down, "Budd" because of Izzy's name, Rose. Tuck Budd.

"Do you hate us?" Izzy asked when the story was over.

Then I couldn't help it, I started to cry too. I could hear Herby's violin playing inside of me and it made me cry even more. I said good-bye in my heart to Calvin or Clay or Griffin. I thought about

Izzy as a man as a sun at the Pink Ginger with Anastasia. I thought about Izzy as a man as a cuckoo clock making Uncle Hansel laugh. I thought about Izzy as a boy living in the yellow house with Herby and Molly, not letting anyone take his picture, except once, so there would hardly be a record of who he had been before he changed. I thought about Irving Rose dreaming of becoming Izzy Budd—dreaming of growing that red hair to his waist, dressing up in high-heeled shoes and lipstick, performing on the stage in New York City, raising his daughter. One thing Irving Rose and Izzy always had in common was me. Both of them wanted me, no matter what.

"I love you both," I said. "Even if I wish you were a little more like normal parents. And Molly and Herby would love you if you let them. I love you all. Anastasia and Izzy and Irving, too."

I love you all.

Izzy and Anastasia put their arms around me. "We love you, Tuckling," said Anastasia. I realized then how long it had been since I'd heard my mom's voice.

Tuck Budd—that's me. I live with my family: Izzy and Anastasia. Anastasia talks a lot more now.

Sometimes my grandma and grandpa Molly and Herby come to visit us. I like to dance for them. One dance I do is called "True Body." Izzy and Anastasia and Molly and Herby and I walk all over the city, finding angels, unicorns, mermaids, winged horses. Finding dragons. I believe in all those things. Because I think they are beautiful and even if nature didn't make them, they still exist. In Manhattan, where Izzy and Anastasia and I all live.

Girl Goddess #9

editors' notes:

welcome to girl goddess #9. because of all the letters we've received asking about how we got started, we want to dedicate this issue to that story. it's pretty cool. so here goes. enjoy.

who we are:

lady ivory (formerly known as emily)
hair color: currently, orange. it's been green, blue, platinum. before that i can't really remember.
fav music: bowie, p j harvey, nirvana, hole, sonic youth, patti smith, edith piaf.
fav pastimes: writing girl goddess with alabaster duchess, putting on music really loud and dancing around my room in my silver platforms from the 70's, reading poetry, having picnics in the backyard when the moon is full.
fav movies: the boy with green hair, the decline of western civilization, juliet of the spirits, the hunger, the little match girl.
fav food: green m&ms, cheese pizza.
least fav thing: racism, prejudice.

alabaster duchess f.k.a. anna
hair color: ebony.
least fav thing: people who eat meat, people who make fat jokes, people who are mean.
fav food: peanut-butter-and-marshmallow sandwiches.
fav thing to do: girl goddess, make up recipes, hang out with lady ivory, listen to music.

fav music: tori amos, sara maclachlan, cocteau twins.
fav movies: fantasia, cocteau's beauty and the beast, a midsummer night's dream, romper stomper, nosferatu, an angel at my table, wings of desire.

the first zine

we were in love with nick agate. his album white goddess is awesome. he read this cool book called the white goddess by robert graves and it's all about poetry. it says that real poetry is all based on this old myth about this beautiful, scary, trippy goddess who the poet wants to possess but he always loses her to this shadowy other guy. the goddess is sort of death as well as birth and life. robert graves says that real poetry makes the hairs on your body stand up and that's how you know! so all the songs on the album are about trying to get this lady who could be your own death. it's out there.

anyway, we named ourselves from songs on the album about the goddess. and then we thought we had so much to say about the music and about everything so we got together one day and started writing and that's how girl goddess #1 was born.

we wrote all about the stuff we love and hate and illustrated it with our sketches and photos and pictures from our old fairy tale books from when we were kids, old encyclopedias, old fashion magazines that we messed with. we wrote about vegetarianism, the new feminism, body image, hello kitty and anais nin and the dalai lama, about newt, neo-nazis, pro-lifers and a.i.d.s. we gave hot-line numbers and encouraged our readers to write to us about the things they loved and hated.

(you can reach us at girl goddess box #242, 12358 ventura blvd, studio city, ca 91604)

we sent girl goddess #1 to our favorite writer, isadora pavlova klein, who wrote the coolest book in the world, swizzle kiss.

<u>our review of swizzle kiss</u>

swizzle kiss is kind of a weird name for a book but once you read it you just think its great. swizzle kiss is this funky chick who leaves home and finds her true identity as post-punk-super heroine. she has all these wild adventures kind of like alice in wonderland, another of our fav books. swizzle kiss has pink hair and a heart-shaped birthmark. she rescues her friends from the evil clutches of villains. we love her.

we loved swizzle kiss so much that we sent a letter and girl goddess #1 to isadora klein's publisher. we got a really sweet letter back from isadora klein saying how much she loved girl goddess.

here is the letter:

Dear Lady Ivory and Alabaster Duchess:

Thank you for your super-zine girl goddess*! I love it! I wish that I had friends like you when I was fourteen. I would have been much happier if I had had a zine to work on.*

I'm so glad you like Swizzle Kiss*. I never dreamed so many people would relate to her. I guess it proves that if you write about what gets you going other people will be into it too. So I'm so happy to see that you are plunging into what you love in* girl goddess.

I can see how much you love Nick Agate. I think his music is cool but I have to admit I'm not as much of a fan as you are. To tell you the truth I think he's a little scary. But then maybe that's because I'm getting old. I would probably have written odes to him when I was in junior high and more easily charmed, which is a lovely quality.

Would you be interested in sending a copy of girl goddess *to Nick Agate? My friend Darby Lawn-Jones at* Off-Record *magazine knows him and would be happy to send one along. Let me know if you're interested.*

Thanks again for understanding Swizzle Kiss.

Best wishes,
Isadora Pavlova Klein

we were blown away. of course we were interested and we sent another girl goddess to isadora. then the off-record guy wrote us a letter.

Dear Lady Ivory and Alabaster Duchess:

Isadora Klein sent me a copy of your zine, girl goddess, *which I really enjoyed. You are very talented. It is good to see that you are into hello kitty, the pink panther and fairy tales but that you also appreciate the serious issues that are plaguing our world. I think it's important that you let older people know that your generation understands about darkness and magic, which is, I'm sure, one reason why you like* Swizzle Kiss, *one of my favorite books even though it was published for teenage girls and I am a 32-year-old man.*

I have taken the liberty of sending my copy of girl goddess *on to Nick Agate whom I've interviewed for* Off-Record. *Nick has expressed interest in what girrrls are doing with zines and since* girl goddess *is one of the best I've seen I thought he'd enjoy it.*

Good luck.

Sincerely,
Darby Lawn-Jones
DLJ/cm

nick agate would hold girl goddess in his glowing marble carved hands! we thought we were going to die.

a few weeks later matt-the-rat at k-kil announced that nick agate was going to be playing at the amphitheatre. we were freaking out because neither of our parents would give us any money to go and of course we were totally broke—it was even hard for us to afford xeroxing girl goddess—and totally heartbroken. then the rat said they were going to give away tickets. we speed dialed k-kil nonstop for three days but we didn't win.

then one day we were feeling really depressed. our goofus math teacher moved us apart so we wouldn't talk during class. our slurmoid english teacher gave us a C- on girl goddess #1 which we had been lame-ditz enough to turn in as a creative writing project. some boys teased us on the way home from school. they said something mean about lady ivory's hair, which was green at the time, and alabaster duchess' figure, which is just "too voluptous and womanly and goddess-like for nasty scuds to appreciate" (lady ivory). we went home to alabster duchess' house to make some peanut-butter-and-marshmallow sandwiches and listen to white goddess and hug each other and cry for a few hours. then lady ivory went home. when she got there she found a letter waiting for her on the kitchen table. she started shaking when she picked it up. the return address said, venus records. lady ivory ran into her room and called alabaster duchess. "oh my god! oh my god!" we screamed after every sentence as lady ivory read:

Dear Lady Ivory and Alabaster Duchess:

I'm writing to you in regard to your 'zine, girl goddess. *I represent Nick Agate and he has expressed interest in meeting with you. Perhaps we could set up an interview for your next issue. Nick is often hesitant to give interviews but since your 'zine came from Darby Jones at* Off-Record, *and since Nick was quite impressed with your writing, he has decided to speak to you. We could schedule something on the fifteenth of this month at Nick's private home in L.A. A limousine will arrive to pick you up at 8:30 in the p.m.*

I am also enclosing two tickets to Nick's upcoming concert at the amphitheatre. We'll be in touch closer to the day of the interview to confirm.

Sincerely,
Cliff Shark
CS/flb

the concert

the day arrived when we would be seeing our idol live upon the stage. alabaster duchess' mom drove us in the honda, even though what we really wanted was to arrive in a turquoise-blue studebaker lark or a coral-pink metropolitan. we made up for our mediocre transportation with our stunning fashion sense. we both wore antique white-satin lingerie, steel-toed combat boots and wreaths of white roses in our hair, which we had both bleached white for the occasion. alabaster duchess' mom didn't see the lingerie of course: it was under our black dresses which we removed promptly as soon as we arrived.

the concert was sincerely awe-weaving and mind-unraveling. it is really hard to describe. there were jugglers, panthers, acrobats, naked children with wings, dwarves, a white horse, swine, deer, owls, bats, dancing trees, fireworks, waterfalls, windstorms, twelve-foot-tall flowers growing out of the stage and of course best of all—nick agate. he came dancing out on stilts wearing a devil mask. he huddled at the foot of the stage and whispered and wept.

he pretended to do it with this ghost-type-thing. he stripped off his clothes and dove into a pit of fire. he sang prince of air, consume me, hide the secret, cosmic snake, lady ivory, alabaster and more. at the end all his limbs started coming off. it looked so real that we couldn't believe it was a mannequin that was being dismembered, even when the real nick agate came on stage and took off his mask. we almost fainted in each other's arms, hallucinating that it was nick agate who held us while we closed our eyes.

<u>the interview</u>

due to popular demand we are re-publishing the original interview with tattooed-love-god, nick agate.

nick agate's limo with the tinted windows arrived for us the next saturday at 8:30. the driver wore dark glasses and a hat and kept the screen closed. it was spooky like out of some movie. he drove us up into the hills to (what must remain) an undisclosed location.

there was a giant gate and some stone lions. the gate opened and we drove up the steep path past an orchard of fruit trees filled with lanterns and the sounds of exotic birds. we looked for wild animals that we knew were hiding there but we couldn't see them.

the house was a giant white classical temple with statues of goddesses holding it up. the limo driver stopped and opened the doors for us. he still didn't say anything or smile back at us. creepy! we went up to the front door stumbling over each other. we rang the bell.

a tall man wearing shoes that looked too small like he had stuffed his whole self into them (we only like big chunky shoes) answered. he had one of those haircuts that are short on top and longer in the back. pretty slurmy. he asked us in. he had an english accent. we figured he was cliff shark, the manager.

inside the house was all white marble with red veins. it was lit by candles. there were cages full of wildcats, and trees growing in the middle of rooms and little pools of water built in with lily pads and pretty fish swimming in them. we held hands to keep from falling into one of the pools.

finally we came to this courtyard-type room with a fountain in the middle. it had a statue of a woman washing herself, sticking her hands between her legs and sticking out her tongue. we sat down and this girl who was even younger than us with really pale skin and a pierced nose and wearing a toga brought us lemonade and these french pastry things decorated with white flowers but we were too excited to eat or drink. excited is not the word. it was more like insanely screamingly over the top blown out of the stratosphere.

we waited for a long time. we breathed on each other to see if our breath was okay. we checked our fingernails and discreetly sniffed our armpits. we wanted to explore but even if cliff shark had said it was okay we couldn't have stood up. our legs felt like jellyfish.

then finally HE came in.

he was smaller than we expected but more beautiful. he was wearing baggy white cotton pants and no shoes and NO SHIRT. he had silver rings in his ears, nose, and left nipple. he had a tattoo of a naked lady on his back. she looked like venus from the famous painting. he giggled. "hi" he said. his voice was much higher than we expected. he batted his long eyelashes. he jumped into a hammock in the trees, crossed his legs, put his arms behind his head and said, "shoot."

lady ivory: what's your music about?

nick agate, goateed angel: it's about pleasure and pain. it's about obsession and possession. it's about reaching that peak, going down into total oblivion and re-emerging and transcending. so i guess it's about love.

lady ivory: how did you start?

nick agate, of the piercing star-fire-blue eyes: i was always messing around with music. when i was a kid i'd put on bowie records, dress up in my sister's clothes and run around the house screaming the lyrics. i made everyone insane. i would bang on all the furniture in the house and break plates and stuff, screaming that i wanted a guitar. my mom finally gave me one to shut me up.

lady ivory: what do you think about all this fame you've achieved?

nick agate, wild demon boy: you can't get too caught up in what people think of you. they'll say all kinds of shit. you've just got to do your thing, you know. i've been called a satanist, a vampire, a sado-masochist, a junkie, a fag, a pervert, a freak, you name it. then other people put me up on this pedestal. i just want to write songs that make people's flesh start dancing on their bones without them even realizing what's going on. i want to create something to take you into the fuckin' solar system.

lady ivory: i don't mean to be rude, but i know our readers want to know about the drug thing.

nick agate, lunar deity: the drug thing. do you do drugs?

lady ivory: not really.

nick agate, violent flower: what about her?

alabaster duchess: um no.

nick agate, devil-grin-saint: good. glad to hear it. i don't want to promote drugs. let me put it to you this way, my body can handle a whole lot of shit. my veins are like gold-plated. that's just the way i was born. my gut is like a crystal cave.

cliff shark: i think we better rap this up now, girls.

lady ivory: thank you so so much. we can't even believe we got to meet you!

the magnificent nick agate: does she want to ask me anything?

alabaster duchess: um, yes. what would you say are the qualities that you look for in a lover?

nick agate, the priest of our heart-temple: check you out. good question. i'd say first i look for someone who knows how to love. someone who is strong but soft. i like artists. i like carnivals. i like doing it in fountains. woman is goddess. someday the fucked-up patriarchy will start to value woman. i like someone who makes you feel like they could murder you one minute—i mean, all the way, slit your throat—and the next minute they are nursing you like you are a little baby lamb.

the part of the interview we never printed until now! but now we are going to because we know that girl goddess is the coolest expression of our lovely selves and that we really are girl goddess!

at this time the door opens and standing there is—her! it's the white goddess herself, like in nick's album and in the book. she has long gleaming platinum hair and emerald eyes and red lips and white white skin. she is wearing a skimpy white satin slip, and even that beautiful fabric looks less gorgeous than her skin. we think that compared to her slip our lingerie looks like polyester from sears and compared to her skin our skin looks like the flesh equivalent of a polyester slip. she is barefoot. her toenails look like pomegranate seeds. we can't believe it. "this is celeste," nick agate says. he gets up and goes over to her and gets down on his knees in front of her on the white marble floor and she touches the top of his head like she's giving him a blessing. then she throws back her head and starts laughing and laughing. she looks at us. "who are they?" she asks. "they're girl goddess," nick agate says. celeste starts to laugh again. "girl goddess." "it's the name of our zine," says alabaster duchess. "what are your names?" celeste asks. "alabaster . . ." alabaster duchess starts to say. then she drops her head and whispers, "anna." lady ivory wants to say "lady ivory" but she's not that brave, not when she's standing staring into the face of the most beautiful creature she has ever seen. she says, "emily." "are you tasty?" celeste asks. she looks at nick agate. "are they tasty?" he giggles. "i'm not hungry," she says, sticking out her lower lip. we look around expecting to see the little toga girl with the pierced nose and the pastries but she's not there. "the limo is ready for you, girls," nick agate's manager says.

on the way home, lady ivory and alabaster duchess hold each other and sob. they are crying because nick agate not only is taken, but taken by the most supernaturally gorgeous thing that ever came from the moon to visit planet earth. they are crying because they are not anything like her. they are crying because they want to touch her hair and skin and toenails more than they have even wanted to touch the thin, hard, pale, greek-statue body of nick agate.

and lady ivory and alabaster duchess are crying because they are happy. because they have escaped. because girl goddess will never be the same. because they know, that even if nick agate has tripped from their lives with his

aryan
opium
love queen
goddess-white

upon his arm, there will be a girl goddess #2, 3, 4, 5, 6, 7 and 8. there will always be a girl goddess #9.

thanks for subscribing.
be love because you are.

kisses,

emily and anna (maybe we'll go back to our old names until we can think of something new)

Rave

Her name was Raven but I always called her Rave.

The thing about her was that no matter what anyone said, they knew that she was way beyond them. I was just the only one who would admit it. There are a lot of babes at our school, but there is no one who even came close to her. She had a face and body like some rare French model. Also, she dressed so cool. Really high shoes, those stockings that stop just at the top of the thigh, really short short skirts. Her stuff must have cost someone a fortune—or a lot of someones.

Every morning, a limo would drop her off. Tinted windows, the whole thing. She'd slide out wearing her shades and walk past the stares like she was on a runway. I knew by looking at her that she felt like shit about it though. They all thought she was a freak.

I know about being a freak. When I was a kid

my mom got me into this all-kid rock band. I sang and these other kids played instruments. We were supposed to be a family, but of course it was just this big publicity stunt. We had to do really lame songs. I was only eight, but I sang love songs written for a man. I hated it but my mom wouldn't let me quit. I made her a fortune and she spent the whole fucking thing by the time I was thirteen. It was so sick. I would never put a kid through that. And then they grow up and aren't perfect-looking babies anymore and they really feel like shit. People used to recognize me all the time. They'd think because they'd seen me on TV that they could come up to me and touch me, ask me all this personal stuff about myself, ask for pieces of my hair. It was so weird. Now no one recognizes me. I don't look anything like I used to. My mom would kill me if she knew how much pot I smoke, and the cigarettes and the drinking. Not because she cares about my health, but she'd say that explains why I'm not pretty enough for her to exploit anymore.

Actually, one person recognized me from my band days, and that was Rave. That was how we met. She came up to me in the quad where I was drawing by myself at lunch and she goes, "Weren't you in The Lamb Family?" She didn't mention our stupid hit song that I've been hearing my whole life. She looked almost shy, which surprised me. I remember she was wearing this purple outfit and her black hair almost had a purplish shade to it. I wished I could paint her.

I kind of shrugged and she said, "I could tell by your eyes. I had the biggest crush on you when I was a kid." I hadn't heard a girl say that for a long time. I used to hate it but she sounded sweet and almost sad when she said "kid." Like it was so long ago. Then she tossed her hair, put on that tough mouth again like she didn't want anyone to get too close, so I said, "Don't tell anyone. I don't want to get hounded by autograph seekers." We both laughed for no reason, and I could tell she felt better. She took off her sunglasses and she really did look like a little girl to me for the first time.

We were both freaks. She was because she was a super-groupie who went to concerts and hung out and slept with rock stars who bought her clothes and sent her home in limos. I was because I used to be this little singer and now no one remembers, and if they did they'd say, "Oh what happened to him? He used to be so cute." And what it did to me was it made me not a kid either, like Rave. Neither of us ever felt like kids.

Except together. Which was why we hung out so much. Usually we went to her apartment because her mom was never home. We'd listen to music as loud as it would go and get high and raid the refrigerator, which usually meant we ate those plastic cheese slices on white bread with mayo or ice cream and always Diet Coke because it was the only soda her mom would buy. Sometimes we mixed some rum in with it. We goofed, watched TV, messed around with her Ouija board. Once I asked it a question without telling her what it was and it scooted over to "no" the fastest it ever had.

Sometimes I sketched her but they never did her justice. She liked them though. She put them up on her wall next to the signed posters of all these rock gods and the photos of her with them. I'd look at them and inhale the smoke from the joint really hard. The men on her walls were tall with bulging tight pants and big lips and teeth and long hair all back-lit. Maybe I would have turned into one of them if I'd stayed in the business. I wanted to tell Rave to stop screwing around with these assholes that were using her, but I didn't want to sound like I was trying to control her. That was one thing she liked about me—that I left her alone about it. She wouldn't have listened to me anyway. When she talked about them she got this look in her eyes, the same look she'd get when she was letting the little plastic pointer thing skid along the surface of the Ouija board. She was totally in a trance, transfixed. She looked even more beautiful then. I saw what the rock stars saw. She wasn't some little girl. She was this goddess or this fairy princess, this gorgeous alien super-freak. They thought and she thought that her beauty was because of them, that she was reflecting them back to them, but I knew that she was the one. The beauty was hers, she gave it to them. She animated them with it. I wish I had been able to tell her.

I guess I did, once. It was Rave's birthday. She had this big gig that night—she called them her gigs like she was playing, but it meant she was going to hang out until the lead singer took her home. But that day I asked her if she wanted to do something with me. It was early June; school was almost out. We ditched, and took a bus to the beach. I liked to lie there and bake like I could shed my old self in the sun like a snake. Rave didn't go to the beach much, she was into really white skin. But she wanted to go with me that day. When we got there she asked me to rub some lotion on her. Her skin felt like some kind of material you'd make a girl's dress out of, or like some flower or fruit, but nothing I'd ever touched. Much softer than anything. It was hard to imagine that many men touching it. It was protected still, somehow.

I said, "You're so soft," and she said, "I have a special beauty secret. Rock star body fluids."

"No way, Rave," I said. "By touching you they're getting their power," and she just looked at me. Her eyes got really wet. I saw the tears quivering just at the rim, ready to spill over but she wiped her eyes and laughed.

"You're so nice to me," she said.

"No. I'm a son of a bitch," I said and we both laughed a laugh like salt water and sand on a cut.

"Let's go in the water," I said, and I took her hand and we ran down to the ocean.

"I'm afraid," Rave said.

"You? You're not afraid of anything." And I picked her up—because even though I'm small I have strong arms—and carried her in. She screamed and kicked her legs around. She had the longest legs and her black hair was loose and brushing against my arms and her breasts were pushing out the cloth half-shells of her bathing-suit top. I felt like I was carrying a mermaid or something. She had a g-string bikini bottom and so all of her was in my hands with no material between us. I noticed that some of the paint had peeled off her toenails and it made me want to kiss her even more. I knew she'd go home and fix it before she went out tonight, but she let me see her toes that way.

I didn't kiss her. I remembered this person kissing me, slinging their tongue around in my mouth when I was a kid, and I felt the whole ocean surging up in me. I was afraid of hurting this mermaid who shouldn't have had to walk around in this fucked-up city at all. The rock stars knew it too and tried to buy her sparkling green and silver things to wear and too-high heels and put her in limos. She was so mixed-up, she thought that she didn't belong in the ocean; she was scared of it. But what she should have been afraid of were all those people prowling around on land. And me too. Maybe she should have been afraid of me too. Wanting something from her as much as those guys that could at least give her clothes and hotel rooms with flower arrangements as tall as I was and champagne drinks for breakfast. As much as those people had wanted something from me when I was a cute kid.

So I let go of her, and at first she looked like she was going to grab on again but instead she started paddling a little, and pretty soon she was going for it, watching me and catching waves, bodysurfing, screaming the whole time but digging it, happier than I'd ever seen her and not afraid. She really was a mermaid. She came bursting up through the waves with sparks of light flying off of her and her hair like shiny black seaweed and her eyes like sunken treasure discovered at the bottom of the sea.

After that I bought us ice cream cones on the boardwalk—cherry vanilla—and we walked around eating them. Everyone stared at her like usual but she didn't seem like she noticed it. Her hair was all messed up and all her makeup had washed off in the ocean and she was barefoot, so I was almost as tall as her. While she stopped to get a drink of water this Rasta guy in a wheelchair came up behind me and said, "Your girlfriend is fine, man. You watch out for her." He rolled away before I could tell him she wasn't my girlfriend and that no one could, but I had loved hearing that. I told Rave, and she didn't laugh like I thought she would. She said, "Baby, you take care of me better than anybody," and she kissed my cheek.

It was weird, it was like that was enough for me, like as good as if we'd made love. I was so buzzed from the touch of her skin and the sun and water and creamy sugar and her kiss. We fell asleep on the bus ride home, leaning against each other, warm shoulder to shoulder.

That night, Rave went to a show and stood at the front of the stage wearing a tight shiny emerald-green dress. The lead singer saw her and crawled around singing to her. After the show she slipped backstage—no one had ever stopped her. The singer signed his name on her poster and then on her arm like a tattoo. She told him it was her fifteenth birthday and that she only wanted one thing. He put her in his limo and fed her drinks and drugs in some hotel room and in the morning she got up before him, showered, dressed, woke him up and said, "I might be a groupie but I get straight A's" which was true about her, so he had his limo driver take her to school where I met her in the quad. She told me she had a blasting headache and I gave her a painkiller and we hardly talked. Maybe the day before had been too much because we didn't hang out as much after that. It got less and less all summer. I had this girlfriend and Rave was doing her thing.

Once, I asked her to the beach again. She said, no, she didn't want to get burned.

She dropped out of school a little while after that, and when I called her number it had been disconnected.

I'm in my twenties now, a graphic artist. My girlfriend now is a writer, and she asked me to help her come up with some ideas for short stories about teenagers and I thought about Raven again. I didn't want to hurt my girlfriend's feelings because she is really sensitive; everything makes her jealous, even stuff from the past. But I decided to tell her anyway because I love her so much, and sometimes it's a drag not to be able to share things from the past like that. So I told her, and at first I could tell she was a little uncomfortable that I had kind of worshipped this woman who was so different from her. But when I was finished she had tears in her eyes and she said, "That's so sad. Do you know what happened to her?" I said no. A few days later she showed me the story. It freaked me out because it felt like she knew me so well and it brought Raven back to me as if she were still climbing out of limos in short dresses and with a hangover, on her way to get an A in algebra before she headed out for her next gig.

The weird thing is that just after my girlfriend finished the story, I got a call from the girlfriend I got together with that summer after the day at the beach with Rave. We hadn't spoken in years. We started talking about people we'd known and I asked about Rave, and she got really quiet.

"You didn't hear?" she said.

I said no.

"It's been years now," she told me. "Raven White o.d.'d on heroin when she was seventeen."

I haven't told my girlfriend about it yet. Everything makes her cry. I think about Raven and how almost nothing did, except that thing I said that day, and I wish more things had made her cry and I wish I could have swum just once in the sea of her mermaid tears where all the rock stars should have drowned.

The Canyon

Désirée dreamed of taking the canyon out of the Valley forever. Leaving the blank hot Valley and cresting the hill where the road widened. Winding and plunging down into green. The canyon would pour out then, pour out like a river into the Hollywood sea, and Désirée, probably feeling the beer in her knees by that time, would look out at the mouths on the Sunset Strip billboards, ready to swallow her up, and would want to be swallowed up by those mouths full of song and sex—to be swallowed up by Hollywood.

Désirée lived in a condo in the Valley with Lorraine, who was her mother. All around them was just flat desert. Taco stands and frozen-yogurt places and malls and cars that looked even harder in the sun. The Valley was chain-link and train tracks and used-car lots. The air smelled like tar and the heat made the trees heavy.

Désirée tried to look for beauty in the Valley. But even the pink oleander flowers were poisonous. There was no water in the cement wash that the kids used as a skateboard park. The houses were little low stucco boxes that made your knuckles bleed when you rubbed against them as you walked past.

If there was going to be beauty she would have to make it herself. She slicked her lips as sugar pink as the candy she ate. She smoked St. Moritz cigarettes with gold tips in the school Girls' Room and pulled up her shirt to look at her breasts. During class she sketched dresses—sequined mermaid gowns and ones like feathered paradise birds, dresses like the flowering trees that grew in the canyon. After school the L.A. dees, who were Désirée and Deena and Debby, went to the mall to buy black-lace stockings and the hugest hoop earrings and to see movies starring people with luminous, looming faces in air-conditioned cubicles. Or they went home and lay by the condo pool in the smog, peeking under their bikinis to admire the contrast of the tiny white place hidden there with the coconut-oil sleek brown of their tans.

Almost every night, the L.A. dees went to a teen

dance club because they could walk there and at least it was something to do. They were sitting behind the d.j. booth wearing tight black and taking Quaaludes with their Diet Cokes when the Devil Dogs swaggered in—vicious canines tattooed on their biceps and hair gelled and sprayed into horn-shaped spikes.

"Am I dreaming?" Désirée said. For a minute she was embarrassed to be caught in the Valley, but they were here too, after all. The beauty she had been searching for.

"You've got to be kidding," Deena said.

Debby pointed a finger down her throat.

Désirée was not afraid. She walked over to where they sat at the bar, smoking and scowling, and she asked for a cigarette. All three of them looked at her through the smoke, saw her lit up by the red and green flashing lights—blond hair, cat eyes, small breasts, narrow legs, feet looking strained and naked in her high heels. Dobey took out a cigarette and gave it to her. Then he held out his own and she sucked her cigarette to life.

"Thanks," she sighed, and walked away.

Later, in the parking lot where everyone hung out—drunk, high, not wanting to go home—Dobey came to her with his bleached blond horns glowing against the kohl-dark of his skin.

"Are you going to see Armed Force Saturday?"

"If I could get out of the Valley."

"It's my mission in life to rescue beautiful women from Valley Hell." He handed her a matchbook with his name and number written on it.

Désirée went alone with the Devil Dogs to the gig; she didn't tell the L.A. dees. Dobey, wearing a leather jacket over bare skin, Levi's and engineer boots, picked her up in his VW full of smoke and Rodney on the Roq and Devil Dogs. She sat in front and Rott and Bull sat in back drinking beers.

"You smell good," Rott said, sniffing her neck. She laughed. He was more like a puppy, not even a Rottweiler, but some kind of cockapoo thing.

Dobey got off the freeway in Studio City and took Laurel Canyon, driving down among the palm trees and eucalyptus, cactus, amaryllis and hibiscus, the hillsides of wild mustard and Mexican evening primrose, gardens of phallic, miraculously balanced rock sculptures, the Greek temples and Spanish villas, wood-frame farmhouses, ivy-covered cottages and stone ruins, the nestling restaurant with its Aztec-goddess mural and its scents of basil and roasted garlic, the coyotes and wild parrots, the lanes named Happy, Honey and Lark branching off the stem of the main road like blowsy flowers, the liquor store with its psychedelic sign where they stopped for more beer.

The street in front of the club was crowded with bodies, leather, black Mohawks, bleach-white flat-tops. The Devil Dogs stormed inside. When the music started pounding and cracking they were slamming with their elbows and shoulders and knees, they were flailing off the stage and surging, even off the balconies, and breaking each other's falls. They took turns standing with Désirée and lighting her cigarettes. Dobey asked her to hold his leather jacket. It was heavy and made her arms sweat. When he came back from the pit, he had cuts on his shoulder.

"Some skinhead had a knife," he said.

Désirée took a Kleenex out of her purse and blotted the blood. He looked down at her with smudgy eyes. "Be careful," he said.

After he took Rott and Bull home, he drove her back into the canyon.

"I love it here," she said. "You know, there are

three streets in a row called Happy, Honey and Lark. I want to name my kids that."

Dobey was kissing her and running his hands up her skirt inside her black-lace underwear. Gently, he released the seat. "You okay?"

She nodded.

"All taken care of?"

"Yes, don't worry," she said, pulling his neck down. It reminded her of a stallion.

"But they'd be gorgeous, wouldn't they?" he whispered.

Happy, Honey and Lark. His full lips, her blond hair, dark-honey skin, she thought.

He unbuttoned his Levi's and pushed himself between her legs. She felt a salty, stinging fullness. The city at the bottom of the canyon crackled like an electric carnival.

The next night, Désirée heard someone knocking on her window. She looked out and saw the white hair and the surfboard. Dobey had been surfing in Ventura. He smelled of salt and pot and dirty socks.

"My mom will kill me," Désirée said, opening the window. Outside the sound of crickets was so hot, it seemed to be singeing the June air.

"I mean she will like really kill me."

"But I'll protect you from psychos who climb in the windows." There had been some man breaking into Valley homes and shooting people in the head while they slept. Désirée had nightmares about him all the time. He had a face like a movie-star mask.

Dobey straddled her, easing her down on the small bed that stood among heaps of old *Vogue*s and *L. A. Weekly*s and *Spins*, flyers for bands, lace bras. He started kissing her and biting her neck, and she held onto his shoulders, finding the ripples and hollows of them beneath the damp T-shirt.

After he came, he fell asleep, his face a summer boy's, a kid who's played all day in the water and eaten fruit and fallen asleep with his shirt on and his pants half on and his butt up in the air a little, letting the coolness touch his body while his limbs twitched with the memory of the waves.

The next night, they were taking a swim in the condo pool, late, their legs helpless with water and desire, when Désirée's mother, Lorraine, came out onto the balcony. She was a bloated woman with her hair in curlers.

"What's going on?" she said thickly, clutching her robe to her breasts.

Dobey ducked under the water.

"I'm just swimming, Lorraine. It was hot. I couldn't sleep."

"Well get back in here," Lorraine said. She stood, swaying on the balcony. Désirée felt Dobey struggling under the water. Finally, Lorraine went inside.

"She is totally fucked up," Dobey said, touching the yellow-and-violet bruises on Désirée's arms a few nights later. They were lying in her bed after another swim, their hair still wet and green-smelling from the chlorine.

"I think she's just real freaked since my dad left. She freaks when she sees me with guys," Désirée said.

"Wait until she gets a look at the color of this one."

Désirée started kissing his chest.

"The next time she tries beating on you, you're coming to stay with me," he said. "Maybe I'll have a place by then."

She closed her eyes, wanting to slip away from everything.

In the morning he said, "I dreamed you were standing in this dark place and you touched these dead flowers and they lit up like they were electric or something."

She draped her legs around his waist.

"Electric lilies," he said. "Lighting up the Valley."

All that summer, Dobey and the Devil Dogs came to get her. In the dawn they drove to Zuma and surfed. Désirée learned so fast on their extra board that they gave up teasing her after the first time. She was too vain to wear a wet suit, so she did it in her bathing suit, showing off her perfect glossy thighs. Surfing was easy if she thought of it as being inside her own body when Dobey was making love to her.

On the way back, Dobey stopped at the Santa Monica pier for hot dogs at the Cocky Moon and sometimes they got drunk under the boardwalk, listening to the carousel turning like a giant music box over their heads. Then they stumbled up to the pier and Désirée paid the mechanical fortune-teller, Estrella, to read her future.

"There was this crazy guy who lived over the merry-go-round," Bull said, showing his crooked teeth. "And he killed this chick and stuck her eyeballs into that fortune-teller thing."

"You are so gross," Désirée said, while Estrella's eyes shifted like marbles in her head.

"What a bitch!" Rott handed Désirée his fortune.

Beware, it read.

Désirée crumpled it up in her hand and stuck in another quarter. Estrella's eyes shifted and her hands moved over the cards. A new fortune came out.

Happy travels are in store for you. Désirée tucked the card into Rott's pocket. He grinned.

On the way home they stopped at Frederick's of Hollywood where Désirée tried on purple-lace lingerie and let all the Devil Dogs look into the dressing room, although she pretended she thought it was just Dobey who saw.

After gigs where they shotgunned beers and slammed to bands, the Devil Dogs and Désirée drove home over the canyon, wasted and bleeding sometimes, while the sky started to bleach out, as pale as Désirée's hair. In the Valley, they slept; they woke up thick and sweating and went to Bull's to watch reruns until it was time to go out again.

September came even hotter, so hot that it left a film on your eyes and the backs of your knees when you woke up. The air smelled like sulfur. School would be starting again in days.

"It seems like everyone's dying," Désirée said one night. She and Dobey were lying in her bed, not touching, watching a report about the stalker on the news.

Dobey was silent.

"All these murders. And Missy. And I bet you anything Mark Sand has AIDS."

Missy, who played bass in Armed Force, had shot herself in the head with her dad's rifle in his house in Encino. Mark Sand, who sponsored shows around town, had been the coolest guy in the scene, but he had disappeared. Someone said he had moved back in with his mom in Van Nuys. Désirée ran into him getting a prescription filled at the drugstore. When she tried to hug him, he pulled away as if it hurt, or as if he were afraid of hurting her.

"Doesn't it freak you out that everyone's dying this summer?"

Dobey turned his back to her and pulled the sheet over his head. She hunched around a cigarette and looked out the window at the feeble lights swimming in a mirage sea of heat.

In the morning she woke thirsty, with a clenched feeling inside of her. It was 2:30 in the afternoon. Dobey was gone.

"The Devil Dogs are going out tonight," he said when she called him at Bull's.

"What do you mean?"

"I'll call you later."

Désirée went alone to Deena's party. She was standing by the keg watching girls in pink mini-skirts and plastic jewelry dancing around.

"Where's your boyfriend?" Debby asked, all eye-lashes and cleavage and beer. "Doesn't he like live in his car or something?"

"What's it like sleeping with a nigg . . . a black man?" Deena said.

"What did you say?"

"You know what they say about black guys." Debby tossed back her hair. "You know, they say . . ." Désirée thrust her fist under Debby's rib cage. When she was outside of the gate, she started running down the street.

"L.A. dees," she thought. "L.A. *dies* is the way you should say it, you Valley airheads."

Late that night, while she lay awake, watching a report about the night stalker on the news, she heard a tapping. She tried to move but the hot night was bearing down on her like a body, sticking its tongue down her mouth, holding a knife to her throat.

The window opened. Dobey slid into the room.

"You scared the fuck out of me," she said.

"I'm sorry, Des." He tried to kiss her, but she pulled away from him. Then she saw his face.

"What happened?"

"It's no different anywhere," he said. "There's no place to escape to."

"What happened, Dobey?"

Rott had crashed his motorcycle on the Valley side of Laurel Canyon.

The night after it happened, the two remaining Devil Dogs and Désirée, with her hair like theirs, came to hang a black death banner on the oleander bushes and to swarm up and down with beers in paper bags. As people drove home, they saw the horned faces looming out of the dark at them.

Désirée swallowed mouthfuls of beer and jumped onto the hood of Dobey's VW. A beer bottle crashed and shattered against the curb and Bull yelled, "Fuck!" as he stumbled in front of a car. Dobey pulled him back. He opened the VW door and Bull crawled inside. Dobey covered him with a blanket.

"There's nowhere to escape," Dobey said jamming his hands into his pockets and staring into the Valley.

"That's not true, baby," said Désirée.

She took his hands and pulled him to her, wrapping her legs around his torso. She could feel the sobs in both of them, but quiet, silenced by the kiss.

They could escape inside each other.

Désirée wanted to drive into the dark flowering part of the canyon tonight and light it with the torch of her hair, the torch of her heart. Someday she would have a house there—an old one with a terraced garden of amaryllis, iris and tasseled silk trees, a crumbling fountain, a swingset heavy with children in the evenings, some cats and dogs, a porch full of surfboards, a big kitchen at the center with sand on the floors. She would have friends over and feed them barbecue and strawberries and play music until everyone fell asleep on the couches and the cushions. She would have Happy, Honey and Lark, breathlessly beautiful with their flame-pale hair and charcoal-dark skin.

Désirée wanted to drive deep into the canyon tonight, to camp in some deserted garden shrine. There were some pink amaryllis left and the grass smelled of summer, even though the summer was over.

Pixie and Pony

Pixie and Pony are going to the prom. They are wearing pale-pink moiré taffeta minidresses. Pixie bought hers at a boutique on Melrose where she and Pony like to shop on weekends. Pony made her dress; she can make anything, Pixie thinks. She feels proud to be matching Pony and knows that the Pony-made dress will look better than anything anyone is wearing.

Pixie wishes that her father would take a photograph of her and Pony in their prom dresses. He has taken pictures of them together since they met in second grade. He used to drive Pixie crazy, making her and Pony stay still for what felt like hours until he got the right shot.

"You two look like flowers," he would say, setting up his camera in the garden.

Once he took their picture sitting in a tree.

"You look like dryads."

Tonight Pixie wouldn't mind posing for him for hours. But he is sick. Pixie tries not to think about it. At the prom she will get a photo taken with her date, Leonard. She might bring it to her father in the hospital.

Leonard is a skate punk with a broken nose, a Mohawk and bright-green Creepers. Pixie met him at a dance club in the Valley. They won a fifties dance contest together. Pony's date, Romeo—he swears that is his real name—is gorgeous and Italian-looking; he also has a Mohawk and Creepers. Romeo is wearing a red-plaid kilt over his tuxedo. Pony met him at the market where she worked one summer. He takes her to punk shows in Hollywood on the back of his motorcycle.

Pixie and Pony and their dates are in a rented limo on the way to the prom. Pony's friend Mini and her date, Snack, are in the limo too.

Snack is the only male in the limo, besides the driver, who doesn't have a Mohawk. He is a surfer with blond curls and gleaming white teeth. His blue eyes look crazed from the coke he has been snorting. Mini has a face like a cherub and long blond hair; she won "Best Body" in the school yearbook. She and Pony always dress up in matching clothes. They call each other each night and discuss what they will wear the next day. They wear minidresses and bondage jewelry or ripped jeans with crop tops and animal print Creepers. Pixie wishes she could always match them too. Tonight, like Pony and Pixie, Mini is wearing a pink taffeta minidress that her mother, who is a fashion designer made for her. Pixie secretly wishes that for once just she and Pony could be matching and not Mini.

The prom is at the Beverly Hills Hotel, which is pink like the dresses. The three couples get out of the limo and go inside. Everyone turns to stare at them, of course. They take their time getting to the table so everyone will have a chance to look. Pixie forgets about wishing that just she and Pony were wearing matching dresses. She feels proud to be with Mini, too. Besides, she and Pony are the only girls there with Mohawked dates.

When the music plays, Pixie and Leonard, Pony and Romeo and Mini and Snack start slamming even though it is not punk rock, of course, but some geeky pop thing. They lope around swinging their elbows and kicking their feet. Everyone stands back. The teachers look like they are going to break it up but they seem a little scared. Only when the three boys start going at it, slamming really hard, do the teachers step in. Pixie, Leonard, Pony, Romeo, Mini and Snack are thrown out of the prom before they've had the chance to eat the pressed-turkey dinner and defrosted vegetables. They don't care. The only bad thing is that they didn't have their pictures taken. Pixie tells Pony she wants one for her dad. So Pony sets up her camera with the timer and takes a picture of all of them crammed together in front of the hotel that is pink as a prom dress, with the palm trees like punks with long necks growing all around.

Then Romeo, who is older, buys champagne at a liquor store and they go to Mini's house in the hills. Mini's mother is out. They sit in the Jacuzzi guzzling champagne and passing around cartons of ice cream.

Later, Snack and Mini pass out in the living room.

Leonard and Pixie have wham-bam sex in Mini's mom's round bed under the mirrored ceiling. Pixie feels where there will be bruises on her thighs tomorrow.

Romeo tells Pony he has to get home.

Leonard leaves a little later.

Pixie goes into Mini's room where Pony is sitting on the water bed against the polka-dot vinyl wall. She looks like she's been crying. Pixie thinks Pony is the most beautiful girl she has ever seen—thin and brown with tawny wild hair.

Pixie remembers how they met in second grade. She noticed the skinny girl with pigtails drawing a picture of a horse. It was so good Pixie was immediately jealous and awed. Pony's long thin fingers covered with rings from all over the world could do anything. They had made tiny hats for the bears that lived in Pixie's dollhouse and a pair of spectacles with real lenses of clear nail polish for the father bear. In junior high Pony's hands had made a family of perfect ceramic horses. In high school they had made a pink velveteen fringed minidress for Pixie's seventeenth birthday. Best of all Pony's hands, and the rest of her, could take photographs. Her parents had taken her to West Africa and Mexico and Pony had photographed children. She had also gone to Watts and taken pictures of children there. In every picture you could see Pony, even though she almost never did self-portraits and hated anyone else to photograph her. But you could see her in the dazzled eyes of the children, Pixie thought. Pixie loved the pictures. They were full of sad, beautiful details—a small flower in a child's hand, an empty bowl, a dead bird.

"Are you okay?" Pixie asks Pony now.

Pony nods. "He told me he has to get home to his girlfriend," Pony says. "I didn't know he had one."

Pixie wishes that Pony wasn't going to be going away to school in a few months. It will be strange, after eleven years, to not know what Pony is wearing every day, to not be able to hand her notes between classes and call her every night. To not be able to go running and shopping and dancing together. To not be able to talk about boys or to know who Pony's new friends are.

Pixie has always wanted to be best friends with Pony. In elementary school, Pony's best friend was a tall, athletic girl named Cara. Pony and Cara went horseback riding together after school and on the weekends, or their mothers drove them to the beach. Pixie was afraid of horses and hated the idea of using a whip; she always got bad burns when she went in the sun.

Once Cara and Pony hid the brown paper bag lunch Pixie's mom made for her every day. Pixie, who cried easily then, cried. Cara laughed and called Pixie a baby. Pony didn't say anything. Later, Pixie and Pony kicked each other in the shins and screamed. Neither of them had ever seen the other like that before. It took them months to get over the image of each other's snarling face.

In junior high, Pony's best friend was an olive-skinned girl with shiny dark hair, long to her waist, and strong legs. Maria was an ice skater. She and Pony went ice skating at the mall together every day after school. Afterward they went to the May Company cosmetic counter and sprayed perfume on their pulses while they sucked on sodas. Maria got Pony started on drinking diet drinks, which Pixie thought was stupid because Pony was so thin to begin with. She told Pony, who got mad and said she liked the taste of diet better. Maria wanted to be a veterinarian when she got older. She was very quiet and never spoke to anyone except Pony and her animals. She didn't even speak to the herds of boys that had crushes on her. Pixie sometimes ate lunch with Pony and Maria, but Maria made her nervous because she never responded to anything Pixie said. Once Pixie told Pony that she got creeped out by how quiet Maria was. Pony said Maria was quiet like a beautiful animal and she liked that. Pretty soon Pixie stopped seeing Pony as much but they still passed each other notes or spoke on the phone at night.

Now, in high school, Pony's best friend is Mini. Mini is always nice to Pixie but they don't have that much to talk about. Mini loved to horseback ride when she was in elementary school and she ice skated in junior high. She gets perfect tans even though she is blond. She drinks diet sodas even though she has a perfect body, the "Best Body."

Even though Pixie has never been Pony's best friend, they have always done things together. When they were little kids they would walk over to Pixie's house after school and play in the garden of mint, rosemary, lavender, miniature pomegranate, pansies and Johnny jump-ups. They tied Pixie's mother's scarves around their heads and put her silver bracelets on their arms and pretended to be gypsies, setting up camp, shaking the tambourine, making stews out of mud, flowers and herbs. Sometimes they borrowed Pixie's mother's kimonos and put their hair in buns and had Japanese tea ceremonies with the blue-willow tea set among the irises under a shady tree. They liked to build miniature cities with moats and castles and gardens in the mud. They decorated and redecorated Pixie's dollhouse, covering the walls with scraps of wrapping paper and making mirrors out of tinfoil, dressers out of stacked matchboxes. Once, on Pixie's birthday, they had a peach party in which they both wore peach French T-shirts and peach jeans and made peach ice cream with Pony's mom's ice-cream maker and a peach pie. Pony gave Pixie a T-shirt with a peach-silk peach appliquéd on the front. Of course, Pony had appliquéd it on herself. When it was time for Pony to go home, her mom came and saw Pixie and Pony crouched next to each other, drawing a beautiful forest with chalk on the pavement in Pixie's backyard. They pretended not to see Pony's mom. She pretended they really hadn't and went off to do some errands for a while.

In junior high, even though Maria was Pony's best friend, Pixie and Pony did all kinds of things together. Sometimes one of their moms would drop them off at the museum where they would spend hours staring at the Egyptian statues and Italian frescoes. Pixie thought Pony looked like an Egyptian queen. She imagined her sitting on a barge among lotus blossoms. Pony made sketches of the Italian frescoes. When she got home she would decorate the furniture in her room with wreaths and urns of flowers, fruity vines and dancing figures. Pony's parents always encouraged her to paint on anything.

In junior high Pixie and Pony shared a mutual obsession with Chemin de Fer jeans and went shopping for all the styles—the sailor ones with the panel of buttons in the front, the tuxedo-backs with the little buckle and the lace-ups that tied like shoes. They invented elaborate, sugary dessert recipes which they scarfed up, and then burned off by sprinting through the hills. They made their own magazines in which Pony took all the photos and Pixie wrote the stories. The model for all the fashion photos was Maria. She wore clothes that Pony sewed for her. Pixie described them with words she read in *Vogue* like "luxe" and "chic." There was also an art section with Pony's photos of children. Pixie wrote poems to go with them. Even though they seemed to be about the photos, all of the poems were just as much about Pony, whom Pixie saw in each one. The magazines also had lots and lots of lists: lists of the ten best albums to have with you on a desert island, lists of the cutest musicians, things to do when you were sad ("take a bath! dance! buy a new pair of Chemin de Fers! write your own magazine! make a pink cake shaped like a piggy and have a pig party!").

Pixie and Pony had gone through a stage where they were obsessed with pigs. On Pony's thirteenth birthday they did just what they wrote about in their magazine and made a pink cake shaped like a pig's head with a smaller round cake on top for the snout. Pixie gave Pony a white T-shirt with tiny pink pigs on it.

Once, as a surprise, Pixie dressed up in a pig costume and visited Pony at the store where she worked bagging groceries. Pony was mortified and pretended not to know Pixie. Pixie left crying. Pony called her when she got home and asked her if she was okay. Pixie apologized for embarrassing her. The pig obsession quickly ended.

In high school Pixie does things with Pony and Mini. Most of the things have to do with boys. Mini drives them in her white 1965 Mustang convertible to the dance club in the Valley where Pixie met Leonard. They wear short skirts and vintage pointed tennies from the 1960's that they have bought on Melrose and they dance together until their hair is completely soaked with sweat. They like to dance together better than dancing with boys because they can be more sexy and free and not worry that the boy is feeling self-conscious. That is one good thing about Leonard who is not embarrassed by anything. Pixie liked his Mohawk and then she liked the way he danced. He knew jitterbug and swing steps and he made them look really cool and punk rock. Now, tonight, Pixie realizes that the Mohawk and the dancing and the prom and champagne were not good enough reasons to have slept with Leonard who never kissed her mouth and left right afterward, but it is too late.

On Pixie's seventeenth birthday, Pixie, Pony and Mini had a party at Pixie's house while her parents were out of town. They invited Snack and two of his surfer friends. They made a strawberry flavored Jell-O mold and stuck Pixie's old Barbie dolls in it with their limbs twisted at odd angles as if they were skanking. They had a food fight and threw Jell-O on the walls. That was the night Pony gave Pixie the velveteen fringed mini that was the color of the Jell-O. Pixie put it on, and she and Pony and Mini skanked together, hoping to impress Snack and his friends who passed out on the floor. The next day Pixie and Pony scrubbed the Jell-O off the walls before Pixie's parents got back.

Pixie, Pony and Mini like to go to the beach in Mini's convertible. Even though she still burns, Pixie makes herself go with them now. She wears sunblock and a straw hat, because when she tried to get a tan like theirs, baking with baby oil, she just blistered. It was so bad that she couldn't go out for two weeks. Pony came over and brought her books from the library, *Vogue* magazines and fresh watermelon juice from the health-food store. Once, she even brought a huge straw hat she had made and decorated with chiffon roses and dragged Pixie out to the movies. Pixie kept her head down and Pony gave dirty looks to anyone who stared.

Now when they go to the beach Pixie is almost as self-conscious of her pale skin as of the blisters she had. Boys at the beach hardly notice her next to Pony and Mini, but she goes anyway. She thinks about how soon it will be when Pony will go away to school and she wants to spend as much time with her as she can.

She looks at Pony now, sad because of Romeo, and thinks, No one should treat you badly. You are a lotus-blossom princess. You should be carried on floats and dressed in golden tissue-thin silk and served wine in goblets. She imagines that after she and Pony graduate from college, they will move back to L.A. They will get houses next door to each other in the Hollywood hills. You will have to take a secret path, secret stairways, to get to them. They will have French windows and will be painted pale lilac (Pony's) and pale pink (Pixie's). They will have gardens with fountains and fish ponds and wisteria vines as thick as trees that the previous owner has braided like hair. Pony will paint all their furniture pale yellow and pale green and rose with flowers and fruit designs and retile their kitchens with bits of broken china. They will go shopping at the farmers' market that is set up every Sunday morning on the streets of Hollywood and listen to the blind Picasso-blue-period guitarist singing in Spanish, his voice almost weeping like rainstorms, burning roses. They will buy Japanese tomatoes, fresh basil and dill, organic white peaches, blood oranges and sweet peas. They will go to the ashram hidden in the hills and buy incense. Pixie will make them couscous with pine nuts, rosewater, dried cranberries and ginger for dinner. In the mornings they will go out for guava-cream-cheese pastries and carrot juice at the tropical bakery. They will run in the hills at twilight. They will find two boys, possibly with hair dyed great colors, or maybe just normal hair, but definitely the boys will be thin, sad-eyed artists. Pixie and Pony will have daughters at the same time and let them play with their old dollhouses and rhinestone jewelry.

"I am going to miss you so much," Pixie finally says.

"I'll miss you too," says Pony. She dabs her eyes with the Kleenex Pixie hands her. "But we'll always know each other."

Pixie nods. She sits down on Mini's shag-carpeted floor and stares out the glass doors at the glowing blue pool. The night smells of chlorine, jasmine, Snack's cigarettes and Mini's sweet perfume.

"Isn't it funny?" Pony says. "That we've known each other all this time? We've known each other forever. And we're exactly the same size."

Pixie thinks that they aren't the same size. She feels much shorter and heavier than Pony even though people have said that they are the same.

"And it's weird that we have the same taste in everything," Pony says. "In art and books and food and clothes and music. Why do you think that is?

Is it nature or nurture? I think we'd be the same even if we just met now."

"Me too," Pixie says. "But also you influenced me a lot."

"You influenced me too," Pony says.

Pixie thinks it is unusual for Pony to be talking this much. She usually is pretty quiet about her feelings. Pony reminds Pixie of Pony's dad, who always seems a little distant and cool. Maybe it is because he is so tall, literally distant, and because of how handsome he is. Pony is a lot like him. Even though he doesn't express his feelings much, you can see in his eyes how much he loves Pony.

"I keep picking them, don't I?" Pony says.

"Romeo is a shithead," says Pixie. "He should treat you like a lotus-blossom princess."

Pixie's dad is not tall or handsome like Pony's dad. He is older than the other fathers and a little overweight; his hair is always a little messy, but when he smiles and tells his jokes, or when he plays the music he composes, pretty young women become infatuated with him. His eyes twinkle and his hands are warm and elegant-looking. He tells Pixie all the time that she is his princess, his flower fairy of the garden, his pumpkin. Or he used to. Now he is in the hospital with cancer.

"Maybe it has something to do with my dad," Pony says. "It's like I've never felt he's all the way there for me."

"He loves you so much, though," says Pixie.

Pony nods. Then she looks worried. Her brown eyes big with worry. "Your dad will be okay," she says. "He loves you so much too."

Pixie thinks about the best friend thing. She realizes she is getting a little too old to think about best friends, but she can't help it. She hasn't gotten it out of her system. Maybe if her dad weren't sick or at least if Leonard had kissed her on the mouth or something, she wouldn't care so much.

Pixie says, "Maybe its because of my dad or tonight or because you are going away but I keep wishing that we were best friends. I know it sounds stupid and like a kid but I think about it a lot."

She turns and looks at Pony who is sitting regally on Mini's water bed as if she is Nefertiti, especially with the smudged kohl around her eyes and the snake bracelet on her thin arm—Nefertiti on a barge drifting through the lotus blossoms. Pixie is hoping, trying not to hope. She knows that Pony doesn't say her feelings too often.

"Best friends?" Pony says. "We are sisters," says Pony.

Winnie and Cubby

The air smelled like muffins baking and about to burn and the man's voice on the radio sang sweet and hoarse, full of longing. Cubby drove his yellow Karmann Ghia over the bridge into a city that seemed made of honey and charcoal.

Winnie thought that she was probably the happiest she had ever been in all of her seventeen years. She never had to go back to high school. Michael Stipe was singing "This one goes out to the one I love," followed by an unintelligible wail." She was in love with the hottest skateboarding guy in life and they were going to spend a whole weekend in San Francisco.

There was nobody like Cubby. He could fly on his skateboard. He had heavy-lidded blue eyes and soft lips that made him look like the angels in Renaissance paintings, and he could draw Renaissance angels, cars, portraits and almost anything else. He wanted to go to Italy to study art. He was tan and wiry and he knew the names of flowers; he could dance. Animals always came over to him first. He wore the best chunky puppy shoes instead of the narrow weasel shoes that some guys wore.

Winnie and Cubby had been going out for a year. They met at a party at the end of last summer. The air smelled like beer and trees and had the beginning creep of chill that told everyone school was going to be starting soon. Winnie was drunk on keg beer. She saw Cubby and started dancing by herself nearby, whirring like a frisbee. When she was dancing Winnie felt the safest, as if no one could hurt her. Cubby danced too. He could do things like falling into splits and spinning on his back. He and Winnie jammed and slammed, hip-hopping until it was light. Then they went to the beach and she sat huddled in a woven Mexican blanket while he surfed. They ate whole-grain pancakes in a natural-foods place, and Cubby laughed because Winnie could eat as much as he could even though she was even tinier than he was. Winnie didn't want the time with Cubby to end. When she had to go back to her house she felt the stone of loneliness sinking down through her body again. She had forgotten about it since she and Cubby started dancing.

During the whole school year Winnie and Cubby were always escaping together to skateboard, play pinball on the pier, eat poppy-seed cake, look at art books, just to drive and drive listening to music. After a while they told each other what they were trying to get away from.

Winnie said, "Our house is like a tomb. It's like my mom died when he did."

Winnie's dad was killed when she was twelve. He had been an architect and built their house by the sea. He had also built Winnie huge, turreted sand castles and called her his mer-baby and given her shells and showed her how if you put them in water all their original brilliant color came back. When she cried he let her listen to his magical conch, told her to take three deep breaths and promised she would fall into a sleep of beautiful deep-sea dreams. It always worked.

Now there was just her and her mom and whatever new boyfriend her mom brought home that night.

Cubby said, "Your dad probably is still around you in a way. I believe in that stuff. Maybe he's like your guardian angel."

Winnie knew what he meant. Once, she had been driving home from a party drunk and her mom's car spun out and careened across the street, but she wasn't hurt at all and the station wagon was only scratched. That was one time she was sure her dad had been around. She never got behind a wheel drunk again after that.

She wished she could have been her dad's guardian angel on the night of his motorcycle accident.

"At least you had a father who really loved you," Cubby said.

"Tell me about your dad."

"He's a bastard."

Winnie ran her fingertip along the lines ridging Cubby's forehead.

"He'd back up the car to the edge of a cliff with me in the backseat. I was like three. He'd just crack up when I screamed."

"Oh God."

"And he did things like he told me he and I were going to Europe. He packed my bags and everything. I think I was five. All I really wanted in the world was to go to Europe and see the paintings like in the books. He dressed me up and we went to the airport, right to the gate. And then he starts laughing and saying it was just a joke."

"That's sick. What did your mom do?"

"She didn't know about it. I didn't tell her."

"Why?"

"I don't know. I didn't want to upset her. He beat me up too. He broke my arm once. I told my mom I fell down skateboarding. After that I wasn't afraid to do anything on my board."

"Cubby." She saw a flash-image of her dad on his bike, eyes hidden under dark glasses, square jaw, hands gripping the bars. She froze the picture there.

"And then he left. Thank God. I think the reason I can never stay still is because of him. I read that guys who don't have strong father influences feel like they're spinning all the time."

"I wish I could be your dad," Winnie whispered into Cubby's hair.

"We can be each other's dads."

They were also each other's moms, making sure that the other had eaten, was dressed warmly enough. Once, while Cubby was teaching Winnie to do a special skateboard jump he said to her, "You're the son I never had."

She loved that. It was better than if he said, I love you.

They won "Cutest Couple" in the school yearbook. They went to the prom in matching baggy black tuxedos. Cubby gave Winnie a corsage of orchids that was almost the size of a centerpiece and must have cost him a week's pay from the skate shop where he worked. He said, "Let's drive to San Francisco the day school gets out."

The first place they went in the city was a tiny Japanese restaurant without a name. A line of people were drinking beers out of paper bags while they stood outside on Church Street waiting to get in. Cubby asked two handsome men in very soft-looking sweaters if they would purchase some beer for him and Winnie. The men smiled and one of them took Cubby's money, went to the liquor store on the corner and bought two huge Sapporos. He handed the two paper bags to Cubby. The beers were pearl-dripping with cold and the caps had been opened but half-stuck back on. The man gave Cubby his change.

"I think these big ones cost more than that," Cubby said.

"It's okay," said the man, looking into Cubby's eyes.

"Thanks."

Winnie scraped her finger on the edges of the bottle cap as she pulled it off. She shivered as the cold, dark beer poured out of the glass into her mouth. She felt her whole body soften.

The restaurant was so crowded and small you could hardly walk inside. There was a mural of shy Japanese women peeking out from behind their fans and under their parasols. Some of them were holding babies. The tea smelled sweet, like brown rice. Winnie and Cubby ordered hot miso soup, spinach with sesame sauce and monster-size California rolls—seaweed cornucopias of fish and thinly sliced, flowery vegetables.

After dinner they walked along Market Street for a while. There were packs of men everywhere. They reminded Winnie of the view of the city from the bridge—beautiful, self-contained, remote. She tried to imitate Cubby's loping boy walk so that she could fit in better.

"Let's go in here," Cubby said.

It was a leather store. There were all kinds of black-leather clothes—tight pants with laces, chaps, halters, studded, zippered motorcycle jackets. Winnie tried on black-leather shorts but her zipper got stuck. Cubby had to come in the dressing room to help her.

"Close your eyes, though," she teased.

"How can I do it if my eyes are closed?"

They were both laughing so hard they thought the slim man with the pierced eyebrow would throw them out. Instead he grinned at Cubby and said, "Why don't you take a look downstairs."

The basement chamber was full of spiked things, rubber things, leather things that Winnie had never seen or even heard of before. Cubby teased her, but then he took her hand as they went back upstairs and bought her a black-leather rose which he pinned to her jacket.

They drove to the Haight. The street was lined with stores selling used Levi's, leopard coats, platform shoes, engineer boots, CD's, cappuccino. All of the telephone poles and streetlights were plastered with flyers for different bands. Kids were hanging out everywhere. Winnie and Cubby gave change to a skinny, big-eyed girl who looked like a kitten. Winnie wished that she and Cubby could have a big house someday and fill it up with street kids and cook meals for them and that there would be enough love to go around without anyone feeling left out.

Cubby suggested coffee and sugar. They sat in a cafe getting wired on caffeine and poppy-seed cake. Someone had told them that if you ate poppy seeds your blood would test positive for drugs. They liked to pretend the cake made them high.

When they walked out onto the street they heard music. Winnie thought it sounded like gypsies. They stopped to listen. A musician was playing a violin, moving as if completely possessed. The violinist had café-au-lait skin, long dark curls, a beautiful face and an androgynous body swaying in puff-sleeved midriff top, tight shorts and high pirate boots.

"The most beautiful people are the ones that don't look like one race or even one sex," Cubby said.

Winnie thought about this. She knew that with her short brown hair, square jaw and straight-up-and-down body, her baggy jeans and big shoes, she looked a little like a boy. She thought that Cubby's eyes and lips made him look prettier than she did sometimes. Once, she had put mascara on him for fun and was almost shocked by his beauty.

Winnie pulled his arm. She looked at his face. His eyes seemed far away as if watching a movie, different from the one she saw.

They walked down the street while the gypsy violinist, who was not black or white, man or woman, kept playing, the music clicking its heels and snapping its fingers after them.

Winnie wanted to go straight to the hotel, but then they passed a tiny bar and heard blues coming from inside, and they both knew they had to dance.

The bar smelled of barbecue and beer. They danced in a crowd of people in front of the little stage. As she pressed against Cubby, Winnie thought their two bodies would melt down and merge into one. She thought about this the whole way to the hotel.

The windows of their hotel room looked right out on the still-busy night street, where people spare-changed and cars honked. Winnie went to take a bath. When she got back into the room, smelling of vanilla almond oil and wearing her silk men's pajamas, Cubby was lying on the bed in his clothes, asleep. She kissed his cheek but he didn't stir. She took off his shoes and pulled the covers over him.

"Cubby," she whispered.

He didn't move. Winnie put her arms around him. He was always so warm like a puppy. His light body got so heavy when he slept. She nestled against him and closed her eyes.

As soon as they woke up the next morning Cubby said, "I have to get some caffeine in me."

He kissed Winnie gently with his soft, full, Italian Renaissance angel lips and got up to bathe.

They ate croissants and drank cappuccinos in a café full of overstuffed furniture. The croissants tasted too rich for Winnie and the coffee too strong. She felt queasy and still sleepy. Her head pounded.

"Let's get some sun," Cubby said. He was jittery, his knees jumping under the table.

Winnie and Cubby walked along the Panhandle to the park. Everything was as green as parks on a map. The rose garden was Cubby's favorite. His mother had taught him all the names of the roses, and Winnie quizzed him as they walked the paths in a haze of fragrance.

Snowfire. Sterling Silver. Smoky. Seashell. Evening Star. Sunfire. Angel Face.

They sat on a stone bench and Cubby read out loud to Winnie from *Franny and Zooey.*

Winnie wanted to say, I love you. She could taste the words like frosting on her lips, smell them like the white roses Cubby knew by name.

When they got to Chinatown the shops were just closing. In the window of the butchershop, dead ducks spread and dangled; there was a pig with cherries for eyes. Fish flickered on the sidewalk in plastic bags. The bakery was full of plump pork buns splitting with filling, sticky wedges of rice pastry, glossy, wet, white noodles, flabby on thin paper and sprinkled with what looked like red and green confetti. People hurried out carrying pink boxes that were already staining with grease. Wind chimes and lanterns made tinkling sounds as the shop owners carried them in for the night. The china bowls painted with peonies and queued children, the tasseled hair ornaments, sandalwood soaps and teas in willow jasmine boxes were all swept inside. Everything was lush and lacquered, bloodied and slick with grease, broiled and charred and glazed, basted, steamed, sugared.

In an upstairs Chinese restaurant Winnie and Cubby ordered soup and rice and mu-shu vegetables with plum sauce.

They found a smoky bar. It was crowded with guys in low-slung jeans and beer-belly-stuffed T-shirts playing pool while other guys dressed as women in feathers and sequins watched them. A beautiful black blond in white satin winked at Cubby. Winnie didn't know where to look first.

"I think that angels are like that," Winnie said admiring a redhead in a green sequined g-string.

Cubby said, "I don't think she would consider herself an angel."

"You know what I mean. They are so beautiful. More beautiful than men or women. They're like from another world."

"That's true."

"Why is it that the ideal women's legs only come on men?" Winnie said, admiring some shimmering thighs and calves.

Beautiful men-women. Legs. Lips. Sparkle spangles. After a while it was almost too much. Cubby took Winnie's hand and they started to run.

Winnie was running back to the hotel room, but she felt Cubby running away from the city itself—a glam drag queen with roses in her teeth whose face he did not want to see.

When they jumped on the bed, out of breath, Winnie threw her arms around Cubby and pushed him down on his back. She kissed him. But all of a sudden his body felt cold and rigid. It was like he was someone else; she didn't know him. She tried to stroke his thigh but he shifted away from her.

"What's wrong?"

He shrugged and sat up. Then he said, "I'm trying so hard." He pounded his fist on the bed. Winnie felt the mattress springs contract as if they were inside her body.

"What do you mean?"

"I like guys. I've always liked guys. I kept waiting for it to stop. Or at least to fall in love with someone the way it is with you so then I would have something concrete. But it's just this feeling. I can't make it stop."

Winnie stared at him, his face hidden in his hands. She remembered when she saw her mother weeping, crawling on the floor, calling Winnie's father's name. The feeling of being alone had started then. It stopped five years later, the first time she danced with Cubby.

"How can you tell me this?" Winnie screamed. Her own voice scared her. "I'm your girlfriend."

"If I can't tell you who am I supposed to tell? My mother? The guys I skate with? You're the only person I can tell. What—I should call my father or something?"

Cubby stood up. He looked like a little boy in his multiple-waist-sizes-too-big baggy jeans and backward baseball cap. "Okay, fine. I won't talk about it with you. I should have known you'd act like this," he said. He walked to the door.

"Where are you going?"

"I have to get out of here."

She wanted to run to him and hold him and tell him it would be all right as if he were her child, but he wasn't. They were both just kids. There was nothing she could say.

Winnie went to the window and waited. She saw Cubby walking down Haight Street looking tiny and young. She wanted to shout for him to come back, but she didn't.

All night she sat huddled in the bed. She tried not to move. It was like if she moved her heart would somehow detach and slip out of place, floating lost in the cavern of her body, deflating like a punctured stray balloon. She held up a mirror and looked at her face. She really did look like a boy—a puffy-faced boy now. She wondered if Cubby had pretended she was a boy when he kissed her. She wondered if her breasts made him sick. She hated herself. She wanted her dad.

But Cubby is right, she heard her dad say. Who else can he tell except you? You're his best friend. Maybe you're his only friend. Cubby loves you.

Who else will be able to dance like that? Winnie asked. Who else will give me an orchid centerpiece to wear as a corsage? Who will know exactly which shoes we should both get? Who else will draw like that and ride a skateboard like an angel and read out loud to me?

No one. Just Cubby.

Well. . . .

You'll still have Cubby. You'll find someone else to be your boyfriend. Lots of boys will love you, Mer-baby.

That's almost like saying I'll find another dad.

It might feel that way. Maybe you will find someone else to be like your dad. But that doesn't mean you don't have me.

Winnie lay down. She pretended she was on a beach, listening to the song of a magical conch shell. She took three deep breaths and fell asleep.

Some time after, so late it was early, Winnie heard the door and opened her eyes. She saw Cubby come into the dark room. He stood in the corner.

"What happened?" Winnie whispered.

"I went to a bar and danced with some guys."

"Was it okay?"

"Yes. But I worried about you."

Winnie turned to him. The pillows were still damp with her tears

"I don't want you to leave like my dad did."

"I'll never leave you," said Cubby. "It will just be a different thing."

He moved toward her. It must be the light from the window, she thought, because he was radiant like the angels in his favorite paintings. Maybe it was just because something inside of him had opened up.

"Can I sleep next to you?" he whispered. He sounded so tired.

Winnie felt the sheets stir as his warm body climbed into the bed. She smelled cigarette smoke and felt the rough fabric of Levi's brush against her bare legs.

Then Winnie and Cubby hugged each other, wrapped in each other's arms like little children, until they fell asleep.

Orpheus

"L.A. kills people," Jacaranda said. "You're lucky you're leaving. You'll be able to write."

She looked paler, going through another depression, smoking in bed in her lilac room. The walls were the color of her veins. She was getting too thin, even for the modeling.

Jacaranda died last winter when the flowering trees were bare. You couldn't even tell which ones had once cried the purple blossoms that she named herself after. At the funeral I wanted to read a poem I wrote about her, but I couldn't even speak.

Tonight, I'm at the club where Jacaranda and I used to hang. You take the stairs down beneath the pavement to a room with a low dragon-carved ceiling, red silk-fringed Chinese lanterns, a screen inlaid with peonies, bar of mahogany Buddhas. I'm wearing starry black thrift-shop lace, but even that feels too heavy in the cloying, prickly, woolly heat. All the tattooed-and-pierced ones are hanging out in the red-velvet booths drinking shiny martinis in lotus-shaped glasses or mai-tais decorated like Carmen Miranda hats. I walk around alone and wait.

"You gotta pose for me."

The photographer grabs my arm. He's the one who did Jacaranda's book. His voice is thick like his body. He reminds me of the cigars he smokes.

"Sit there."

I expect him to focus on my face, but instead he calls Mai. She's tall and bony, with heavy black hair against white skin. She digs her nails into my neck and leans on my bare back while the photographer starts to focus. I can feel the tiny moon cuts. I push her away and she goes and clings to him. He blows smoke into her face and arches his eyebrows. I head for a dark booth.

The man who steps on to the stage is delicately formed, small like a child, but his shoulders are broad, his wrists are thick. Gold fireworks of hair falling into his face. Eyes like rooms filled with blue ocean light. Tattered black clothes. He's singing in his scratchy, hypnotic voice, playing his guitar like it's a part of his body, beating on it like a drum sometimes, and even though they're used to the most thrashing bands that drive metal through the fleshy parts of you and etch beats onto your skin, everyone stops and listens.

I remember the night he invited me over. It was so hot that I only wore a white antique petticoat and a T-shirt over bare skin, but sweat was running down my neck and over my breasts by the time I got to his place. The sun was setting as I drove through air thick with pink smog. He lived in an old Spanish building with palm trees growing in front like totems. His room lit with candles. There were bunches of dried wild flowers, ornate crosses, tin angels hanging on the walls above the bed. There were the paintings he had done of Joni, Patti, Sinead, PJ—his goddesses.

He made me soba noodles and vegetables in miso, and we sat on a picnic cloth on the floor and ate the food with a bottle of red wine I had brought. The VCR was playing Cocteau's *Orpheus* with the sound turned off. The pale poet in leather was trying to bring his wife back from the dead.

Orpheus, I thought, looking at the man sitting across from me. When he played his music, then, I felt like a tree uprooting itself to dance, like a flower probed by a bee, opening its petals to sing.

But I didn't dance. I didn't sing.

I reached to touch his lips, his smoky throat, his chest where all the songs first lived. We were kneeling, balanced, poised in moonlight, before we tumbled down the darkness.

He held me all night in the bed. He held me fiercely, not the way I'd expected. As if we had this single night of reprieve before one of us had to go back down forever.

I left before the sun came up, ran barefoot over the wet lawn under the Hollywood sign.

And after that I would wake up alone at night, sit straight up in bed sweating, with his voice pounding all through me. All day I felt feverish and wounded.

It got kind of sick. I've never wanted anyone that much. But it won't happen again, I tell myself. He's as fucked up as I am. Can you imagine the two of us together? Fucking each other up.

But when I see him or hear his voice, even on the tape he gave me, I can't think clearly. I try to understand how I could feel like this, even after a year. A psychic I went to said "soul mates." Jacaranda once said "sex," and then, when it didn't stop—"voodoo." But I think it's what happens when he sings. He touches something—the dream place. The land before it was poisoned. There are untainted fish, unbroken birds, clouds without toxins. Dancing palm trees. Choruses of stargazers. His voice like a god with a lyre carrying us up from the dark tunnel to the edge of the meadow. To the edge of the water. To the edge of the moon.

I try to do that too, but I always feel strangled.

If I could be Joni filling empty rooms with Wurlitzers and silver, baths of blue roses; scream like Patti with the horses rampaging through her veins; like Sinead with her orbit-blue eyes and perfect skull, bringing the elf-lover back from the dead and burying the demon-mother deeper down. I wish I could wear mercury like Polly Jean—landing on the stage from outer space, moving my hands, a cosmic marionette—and make you feel my voice reverberating deep in your pelvis, making you dance, circling your throat like a rosary of tear-shaped beads to press on the glands, to make you weep.

* * *

Now I hear him say, "This is for someone who's leaving soon."

It's a song about the city that's a Sanctuary. Berkeley. The place I'm going. The words seem to pass through me. I want to keep them. I want them.

The song is over and he's standing near the backstage door. Everyone surrounds him. It's hard to tell if they're protecting him or trying to get something. After all, he's the star. Especially now with the record coming out in Europe. He'll be playing Amsterdam soon.

I've heard you walk down cobbled streets with beautiful whores floating above in glowing red windows, green-eyed cat deities perched on sills among the tulips. I've heard you smoke hash as rich as black chocolate. Clubs called Paradiso and the Milky Way.

He sees me and comes over. Pale, heavy-lidded eyes with tiny pupils. Like he's seen visions.

"Hi," he says. He hugs me and I feel his shoulder blades through his damp shirt.

"You were great."

"Thank you. You look beautiful."

People have said we look alike. Small, bleach-blond, boyish. But I don't have the eyes or that voice.

"Thanks."

"When do you leave?"

"Next week."

"It will be good for you there."

In Berkeley the air is different. I will live in the hills, where the air smells the way the light looks reflected in the bay. Sweet violet air at twilight, tangy silver air in the morning before the sun burns through. I will go to campus alone dressed in antique silk slips and beat-up cowboy boots and gypsy beads, and I will study poetry. I will sit on the edge of the fountain in the plaza and write.

"When are you going to read me something?" he asks.

Someday I will come back down here and find him. I will wear white charmeuse satin and a crown of gardenias and baby's breath. I will be barefoot on the stage.

At first I will move stiffly; my hands and throat and feet so cold. I will feel that all I want to do is escape into the coffin, into the silence. I will think of Jacaranda. I will think of him. Then I will begin to speak.

My voice is louder and my heart beats with it and my blood runs with it. My throat opens. I am making white-skeleton junky trees dance and flower. I am bringing lost girls back from underground.

And when it is over he will say, Come live with me above the palm trees, eat chocolate eggs in hotel-room bathtubs, dance like we are making love, make love like we are dancing. Come and stand beside me on the stage, in Paradisos, Milky Ways.

But first I will go away. Somewhere where it's cooler. Somewhere where I'm less afraid.

I will write a book of stories. Of girls becoming goddesses, and goddesses becoming girls. They are all a part of me.

Maybe I will go home with him tonight and whisper the stories in his ear as we lie under the dried wildflowers in a smoky room in the poisonous city that waits outside his window to be resurrected by his music.

But now this girl comes over. I've seen her before. She was in this video for some punk band. She was naked and slaughtering the lead singer in the video. They say you can make blood from ketchup and Hershey's chocolate syrup, but it looked so real.

"Take care of yourself up there," he says. He

kisses me lightly on the cheek, and I touch his wrist.

And he's going up the stairs with the girl following him.

I stand here waiting. To disappear or sing.